HUNTER IN ME

QUEEN OF GATES BOOK 1

LANA MELYAN

HUNTER IN ME

CHAPTER 1

I stopped the car in front of Oliver Hancwell's nightclub. The colorful neon lights from the big sign reflected in the shiny black hood of my '69 Chevrolet Camaro. As the valet rushed toward me, I threw him the keys and headed to the door.

"Hi, Asher," I winked at the bouncer.

"Well, well, look who's back." A wide grin spread across his face. "Come on in." He stepped aside. "Keira?" He bent to my ear as I leveled with him. "We're not in trouble, are we?"

"You tell me," I laughed.

The sound of music hit my ears the moment I passed the threshold and got louder with each step. I reached the balcony railing and looked down at the dancing crowd.

Oliver was sitting at the bar. A young brunette stood next to him, leaning on the counter and playing with his short blond hair with an adoring smile on her face.

The smell of alcohol reached my nose, and I followed it to the bar.

"Dance with me, beautiful." A tall Black guy smiled at me, looking at me with his swimming eyes as I made my way through the crowd.

Returning the smile, I put my hands in the air and passed by, moving my hips to the rhythm of the music.

Trying not to brush Oliver's back, I sat on the stool next to his.

"Here's your tequila," said the bartender cheerfully to the patron at the end of the bar before turning to me. "What can I . . ." His cheer vanished.

"Relax, Bart. I'm not here for you. You didn't do anything wrong. Or . . ." I tilted my head. "Did you?"

"Nope. Just surprised to see you. It's been a while."

At the sound of my voice, Oliver's head jerked to the side. He pushed the woman's hand away and turned around.

"Keira? Hi." He forced a smile.

I nodded.

The brunette gazed at me. She eyed me from top to bottom and then dropped her eyes down again. She released a curt, "Hm," as she fixed her eyes on the handle of a knife sticking out from one of my boots.

"What are you doing here?" asked Oliver.

"Waiting to be served." I turned my eyes to Bart.

"The usual?" he asked. He grabbed a bottle from the glass shelf behind him, put a tumbler in front of me, and filled it with whiskey.

"It's nice of you to stop by," said Oliver.

It was fun to watch him try to act calm.

"Is everything okay here?" I asked, keeping my voice casual.

"Of course it is." He jerked his shoulder. "We haven't had a single accident since your last visit."

I took a gulp from my glass. "Oliver," I sighed, "you have three registered supernaturals working for you. Two vampires—one who is your bartender," I glanced at Bart, "and another your bodyguard. And then there's a witch—Mary—one of your waitresses. Right?"

"Right. And as you said, they're all registered. I'm not breaking any law."

"Right." I gulped the rest of the whiskey and put the glass down with a thud. "Then you've nothing to worry about." I got up, ran my hand under my jacket, and pulled out the gun from behind my belt. "Let's go play some poker."

"Keira, wait," called Oliver as I strode through the crowd toward the poker room.

I came out to a dimly lit hallway, reached the door at the end of it, and kicked it with my boot. The door swung open and hit the wall.

Three of the five players sitting at the oval, green-top table jumped in their seats. The fourth one glared at me and got up. The fifth, a big, broad guy, lazily leaned into the back of his chair.

The first three were humans. The last two were . . . *Demons? Really?*

"You, you, and you," I said, pointing the gun at each of the first three in turn, "get out."

They didn't need to be asked twice, but they took their time trying to collect their money, and that pissed me off. I turned my gun to the side and pulled the trigger. They were gone before the bullet hit the wall.

"Now, you two." I moved forward. "You shouldn't be here."

"Says who?" The big demon on the chair pulled himself up, too.

"The one you're looking at. You blind or something? Don't you see who's speaking?"

"Oh, I see." He smirked. "Silver hair, leather pants."

"Do you see *this*?" I rolled the gun around my finger, then stopped it, pointing the barrel at him.

"That little thing?" His chest shook with silent laughter. "What are you going to do? Shoot me?"

"For starters." I lowered the gun and shot him in the thigh.

His leg twitched, and his laughter turned into a moan.

"Bitch." He sank into the chair, pulled out a knife from behind his belt, and, clenching his teeth, made a cut over the bleeding wound to extract the bullet.

The second demon came at me. He swung his fist, but I crossed my forearms before me, blocking the blow, then bounced and kicked him in the chest. He flew back and crashed on top of the table.

"You shouldn't have come here," I said, my breathing even like I hadn't moved at all.

The guy jumped down from the table and pierced me with his glare. "So you're strong and—"

"And pretty?" I smirked. "Sorry, can't say the same about you." I wrapped my fingers around the barrel of my gun. "Maybe if I fix that crooked nose of yours—" I ducked from his fist an inch away from my face, straightened up, and hammered the back of the gun in between his eyes.

He growled in fury. Squeezing his eyes from the pain, he blindly sent another blow. But I wasn't there anymore.

I darted away when the big guy, who succeeded in fishing the bullet out from his thigh, was about to smash a chair against my head. I thrust the heel of my boot into his wound with a sidekick. He roared, more from being extremely pissed than pain.

"Okay, I'm done being nice." I raised my gun as both of them started toward me. I shot one of them in the foot and the other in the shoulder.

Oliver showed up in the doorway

"Stop," he shouted. "What the hell are you doing?" He spread his hands, staring at me. "If people hear the gunshots—"

"People can barely hear themselves." I rolled my eyes.

"Was that really necessary? Couldn't you just use your magic or something?"

"That would be too easy. Where's the fun in that?"

"Fun? You call shooting people fun?"

"They are not people, Oliver, and you know that. They're supernatural creatures and unfortunately, they heal fast." I pulled out my phone and made a call. "I found them. Send James to Oliver's club." I pushed the phone back into my pocket. "It's your fault they're here," I said to Oliver, putting handcuffs on the big guy who had just extracted the second bullet, this time from his foot.

"This fight isn't over," barked the second demon, pressing his palm to his bleeding shoulder.

"What fight? There was a fight?" With a puzzled expression, I looked around. "Damn, I can't believe I missed it."

"Very funny." The demon glared at me. "Next time you will get what you deserve."

"Really? If you mean a gold medal or something like that, I don't care about those things. You know, maybe a villa on an exotic beach," I said with a dreamy voice. "Or maybe . . . Should I make a list?"

I threw an askance look at him on my way out of the room. As Oliver followed me, I closed the door and pressed my palm to it, locking it with a spell.

I still had to wait for James to pick up the demons.

"How about we have a drink together," I clapped Oliver's back, "while you tell me what exactly you needed those two for."

Atlanta was a normal city, with normal people, who had no idea that the supernatural was real. No one on that nightclub dance floor would ever suspect that Bart was anything but a charming human bartender.

It was our agency's job to keep the supernaturals in order, to catch and deal with the culprits. We were the ones to decide what to do with lawbreakers. It depended on the crime. If they were just intruders looking for some fun, then we would send them back to their realm with a warning. But for serious crimes, we had serious punishments.

Supernatural beings who wished to stay in the human world had to accept their way of living and follow their rules. They were all registered and they knew they'd be watched. It wasn't against the law to recruit them from their realm to work in our world, but the one who hired them had to register the newcomer under his or her name and take full responsibility for their actions.

Oliver wasn't a vampire, or a werewolf, or any other supernatural kind. He was a human who loved his accessories. Knowing things most people didn't made him feel special, powerful.

"I'm listening," I said as Bart put the drinks in front of us.

"Okay, I did. I hired them," Oliver admitted. "I need more guards. You saw what happened last time. The fight, the shooting. Thank God that poor girl survived. But I can't let that happen again. I can't let those sorts of accidents ruin my club's reputation."

It's not people like that girl you're worried about, it's your own big head.

"You can hire humans like other clubs do."

"Humans' senses and reactions aren't the same. They aren't like vampires. They are too slow."

Those are no vampires, you idiot. I decided not to tell him that he hired two demons who only hell knows what they were doing here and who weren't allowed to exist in this world. If Oliver found out, he would take it as a challenge to get one for his collection.

"You already have two vampires and a witch working for you. And because you're a human, you can't have more than three—that's the rule."

"All right, all right." He raised his hands in surrender.

"I'll let you get away with a fine, Oliver, but next time

your money won't save you. If you break the law one more time . . . well, you know what happens to those who annoy me."

I GOT MY ASSIGNMENTS FROM MY BOSS. I COULDN'T STAND HIM most of the time, but a girl's gotta eat, and he was the one who paid me.

When I say pay . . . Well, at least it was enough to cover the rent for my shitty room and buy some junk food.

My work was done for the day, and I could go straight home, but what I found in Oliver's club wasn't what I was expecting.

"How is this possible?" I stared at my boss when I returned to the office. "Demons? Seriously? Richard, how did they get here?"

Richard leaned against the back of his chair and rubbed his mustache. "I have no idea. I've seen a demon only once before. About twenty-five years ago. And that was it. The funny thing is, I always thought demons had horns. But they look just like humans, only bigger." He frowned. "How did you know they were demons?"

"I don't know." I shrugged. "I just knew. And when I got closer, I noticed their pupils. They're only a little bigger than normal, but they're too black and bottomless, like if you yell at them, they'll echo."

"Right. Now," Richard rested his forearms on the table and leaned forward. "The question is, what are we going to do with them?"

"You're asking me?" I pointed a finger into my chest. "How do I know?"

"Well, we have no idea how they got here, and since we don't have a portal to the underworld, we can't send them back." He pursed his lips. "We should kill them. That will be a lesson for the other demons. They'll think twice before crossing to this side."

I rolled my eyes. "No. It wouldn't stop them. What we have to do is to find out where the hell is that hole they came through and close it permanently."

"Brilliant idea. See?" He smirked. "You knew what to do, you just needed a little push."

"What I need is a raise. When I can think less about how to pay my bills and more about my work, I won't need a push."

"How about we get back to our demon problem?" He got up. "Let's go see how cooperative they are."

But the office door opened before he could come out from behind his desk.

"They're dead," I heard James's voice behind me.

I turned around. "Who?"

"The demons. They're both dead."

"And they what," I shrugged with frustration, "both died from a heart attack? They couldn't just die, James. Someone killed them."

"She's right, you know." Richard dropped back into his chair. "Demons don't just die. What happened?"

"I've no idea. After we arrived, I locked them in the cell and left. And I just got a call from the guard that they're both dead."

Richard got to his feet again. "Let's go see what really happened."

The three of us headed to the dungeons. But when we opened the cell and examined the bodies, we couldn't find any wounds or any trace of violence except the bloody marks at the places where I shot them. The demons were just dead.

It was nearly midnight, and after long and pointless speculations, I headed to the door assuring Richard and James that the bodies weren't going anywhere and we could do all this guesswork tomorrow.

I came out to the street, took a deep breath of the fresh air, and headed to my Chevrolet. My car was like my little home, my safe place where I could relax. I got in and slammed the door, leaving the tension of the day behind, then turned on the music and took off.

My empty stomach was making funny noises. All I had today was two protein bars: one for my breakfast and the second for lunch. I took a detour on my way home to get myself a burger.

Washed and fed, I lay on my couch with my half-closed eyes fixed on the screen of my TV, flickering with black and white pictures.

I opened my eyes when the buzzing of my phone woke me up. I glanced toward the window. It was still dark outside. Good news doesn't come from a phone call in the middle of the night, and I hoped that someone had the wrong number.

My heart sank when I picked up the phone and saw my brother's name on the screen.

"Simon?" My sleepy voice came out as a whisper. "What's up?"

"Dad died. You need to come home, Keira."

CHAPTER 2

I was born in New Orleans, the city where anything is possible. The supernatural life is deeply rooted in the city, but of course, not everyone knows it isn't just a myth. Superstitious tourists come to the French Quarter to buy souvenirs or some item that will save them from bad luck or something they're sure is a curse.

Most of them believe that the ones who work in magic shops are fortune-tellers or mediums. But they never suspect that magic is all around them, and the one who just sold them an innocent charm was a real witch, and that same witch is able to pin them to the spot, or turn them blind, or set them on fire in the blink of an eye.

When they bought an artificial blood bag in addition to a cup carrying an imprint of Damon Salvatore's face with blood-covered fangs on it, they didn't believe vampires were real, or, that the man who just walked by could be a real werewolf. No. They didn't. And that's what put them in grave danger.

The rule of three registered supernaturals doesn't apply there. But it doesn't mean if they committed a crime, the creature can get away with it. Every kind has its own faction, and the leader of each faction is responsible for keeping their members in check.

I was a powerful witch, the daughter of the powerful warlock who was the leader of our faction.

As a head of the New Orleans witches, my father used his powers to prevent war with vampires and werewolves and to keep the peace between all species to guarantee people's safety.

Since I was a kid, my father kept me on a leash. That meant he grounded me for using magic in public and had me followed my entire life. He always justified himself by having good reasons for his actions. He just failed to tell me what those reasons were.

I envied normal people. They could do whatever they wanted, go wherever they liked. They could be dancers, designers, constructors, nurses, writers, or teachers. Anything.

Being a witch didn't mean I couldn't be, but only if I had a choice. My father left me none, and when I turned eighteen, I got in my car and drove away.

I decided to be like others. Normal.

First, I found a job in a cafeteria where I had to make waffles. That didn't go well, and I got myself a job in a bar, as a waitress.

But wherever I went, the supernatural followed.

When I saw a vampire feeding on an innocent girl, or a warlock bewitching some teens to do their bidding, I couldn't just walk away. I had to stop them, and the only way to do so was to use magic. And once, I nearly killed someone in the crossfire. An innocent woman.

But I wasn't planning to give up on the chance to have a normal life yet. I just needed more time.

"How much time?" asked Julie, frowning as we sat in a cafe. "It's obvious that this normal, human life isn't working for you." She pushed her empty plate away as she shoved the last piece of her sandwich into her mouth.

"Did Dad send you to get me back home?"

"No. You know he wouldn't do that. I'm doing it because I miss you. You were my best friend and I want you back." She pulled her coffee cup closer. "I need you, Keira. And so does your family."

"What about what I need?" I snapped.

But deep down, I knew she was right. I thought I could do this—have a normal job, a normal boyfriend, live a normal life. But all those normal things were for normal people. And I didn't belong to that category.

But I was used to my independent life and wasn't going to give it up. That was when I started working for Richard. I was older now and I'd learned how to control my powers, but I was still glad that the agency allowed us to use guns and I didn't have to use my magic all the time.

Now, when I look back, I can't blame my father for being overprotective and careful. I was young and too powerful to be set loose, and the older I got, the less angry I was with him.

He taught me everything I knew, including how to control my magic and how to fight. After I ran away, he found me pretty quickly, but he didn't force me to go back. He said *I taught you everything I could, let life teach you the rest.* And with those words, he cut me from the family finances and froze my bank accounts. The only thing he let me have was my Chevrolet, his present for my sixteenth birthday.

I didn't hold that against him either. After all, it was my choice to leave and that was part of being independent, finding my own way.

My own way. The one that now was taking me right back to where I came from.

The French Quarter looked as beautiful as always. And on this warm summer evening, the streets were filled with people and the sound of music came from bars and clubs as usual.

I parked the car in front of the entrance to our house. With a heavy heart, I approached the dark double doors, and it took a moment before I heaved a deep breath and pushed them open.

I walked down the stone-floor passage and came out into our courtyard. My eyes traveled up the old, plastered walls and stopped at the part of the iron railing of the second-floor balcony where my room was supposed to be.

"Welcome home, Ms. Hale," said a male voice behind me.

I glanced back. "Hello, Mike. Is my room still my room?"

"Of course, miss, and everything is ready for you. Clean bedsheets, towels, and all essentials, and if you need anything else, Emily will be happy—"

"Could you get my suitcases from my car and bring them upstairs?"

"At once, miss."

As I started toward the staircase, my brother showed up in the archway of the drawing room.

"Keira? You're here." He hugged me. "I missed you, sister."

"Yeah, I missed you too." I pulled away. "Where is he?" I avoided looking Simon in the eyes.

"In the chapel. You want me to—?"

"No. Not now," I muttered. I wasn't ready yet to face my grief. "It was a long ride. I need to take a shower. Then . . . " As his sad green eyes caught mine, I looked down.

"Yeah, sure. Take your time."

I nodded and climbed up the stairs.

Simon was twenty-six, only a couple of years younger than me, but I always called him my little brother. He was a handsome guy. Tall and well-built, and his hair wasn't silver like mine, but shades of dark brown.

He visited me in Atlanta a few times during my time away from home, but I hadn't seen my father for more than three years.

And that's what made it so much harder. My guilty conscious.

My room looked just the same as before. Nothing was moved or changed. And the moment I walked in, I remembered what it was like to be rich. Never worry about bills, always have a delicious meal on the table and never wonder where it came from. I was never a demanding kid, but I always had the clothes, toys, and pretty much everything I needed or liked.

The door was still open, and I heard Mike come inside. "Your suitcases, Ms. Hale."

"Thanks," I said without looking back at him. "Just leave them there."

As the sound of his footsteps faded, I closed the door, walked to my four-poster bed, and sank on its edge.

I looked at the two suitcases that contained all of my belongings.

After I got the news, I took off at once. I called my boss Richard during the drive and told him I would be gone for a while.

My father was only fifty-seven years old, and he wasn't sick. His death was already as shocking as the untimely passing of a parent could be. But when Simon called and I asked him how it happened, the answer put me in an even deeper stupor.

My father was murdered. And the killer remained unknown.

I didn't come here only for the funeral. I came here to find out who killed my father.

Even when I was a kid, I tried not to cry in front of people, no matter how sad or hurt I was. I hated to be seen as weak. And now, standing next to my father's body in the chapel and looking at his pale, drained-of-life face, with guilt bubbling inside me, I swallowed hard to stop the tears from falling as they pooled into my prickling eyes.

"So how did it happen?" I cleared my throat. "Show me the wound."

Simon moved aside the tie, then unbuttoned the shirt and pulled it away, revealing a mark on Dad's chest. A pentacle with the stars' points sticking out of the circle was burned into his skin right above his heart.

I gasped. "What the hell is that? It looks like a Satan star. Why would someone do this to him? And—" I stared at Simon. "This isn't what killed him, is it?"

"No. What killed him was this." He opened the shirt wider, and I saw three stitched stab wounds on the stomach. "Julie and I examined the mark. The only explanation we could come up with was that the killer, or killers, used it to weaken Dad, and that's how they managed to kill him."

"I don't understand. He was too powerful to be taken down like this. He could sense danger. He was always a step ahead before a werewolf or even a fast vampire could make a move on him. How could this happen?"

"I have no idea." Simon sighed. "I wasn't home that night. Mike called me after he found him dead on the courtyard floor."

"No werewolves or vampires could've done this without a witch's help. Dad never had problems with our witches. He always had their respect. But we can't exclude any of them from the suspects." I yanked the phone out of my pocket and took a picture of the mark. Then I fixed the shirt and the tie and headed to the door. "When is the funeral?" I asked.

"It's tomorrow. I've already made all the arrangements."

I WENT THROUGH MY CLOTHES, BUT FOUND NOTHING TO WEAR TO the funeral.

"I'll have to go to the store. I need a dress," I said, descending the stairs.

"Keira, you're back." Julie entered the courtyard and rushed toward me. "I'm so sorry," she whispered into my ear as we hugged.

"I need to find the one who's responsible for this." I pulled away.

"We're trying to collect some evidence." She spread her hands. "Anything that could help us to figure this out, but there's nothing. Not a single thing to grab onto."

"I'll find something." I clenched my teeth. "I'll shake each and every one of them until something falls out—a piece of evidence, a spell, a murder weapon. Trust me, I'll get you something to grab onto."

"You mean the witches?"

"All of them. All three factions. I'll cut those bastards open If I have to."

Julie and Simon exchanged a worried glance.

"Let's talk about it tomorrow," Simon said softly. "After the funeral. You came a long way. It's late, you should rest."

CHAPTER 3

I couldn't remember when I'd last worn a dress, and shopping wasn't one of my favorite activities. Luckily, I had Julie to help me find the right store and pick the right outfit. It was a black dress with a boatneck and black shoes.

As I was sitting on the ottoman and putting my shoes on, Julie walked into my room.

"Simon is already gone. To make sure everything is ready for the procession." She sank onto the bed. "Keira?"

"Hm?" I got up and looked at my reflection in the mirror.

"How are you doing? Are you all right?"

"Am I all right with showing up after all these years so I can be gawped at while walking in the second line at my father's funeral? Oh, I'm fine," I replied with sarcasm.

"You can do this. Just ignore those judgmental bastards. And they are not all bad, you know."

"No, I don't know. Things have changed." I shrugged. "Not just here. I'm different too. But I think it could be a good thing, you know? Looking at everything with a new, fresh perspective. You're close to them, and you could fish out of them the information needed to solve this puzzle. But looking from the outside, I still might be able to see things you don't."

"True." She nodded thoughtfully.

I gave the mirror one last glance, then said, "Come on, it's time to go," and headed to the door.

As I took my place behind the hearse, I put on my dark sunglasses not only to protect my eyes from the bright sunlight pouring down on us, but also to avoid meeting the witches' curious looks at their deceased regent's runaway daughter. To find my father's killer, I would eventually talk to them, but during the funeral, I wanted to be the one watching them.

Simon gave the brass band a nod, and as the music started, he joined Julie and me.

I saw the representatives of the shifters faction among the people who came to honor my father, and even a couple of the oldest vampires, who were among the few of their kind who could come out during the day.

THE WAKE WAS SET UP IN MY BROTHER'S BAR. SIMON ALWAYS wanted to own one, and my father helped him to get this location and start his own business when Simon turned twenty-three.

It was my first time here, and I liked what Simon had done with the place. The warm brown color of the interior, the wooden bar stools with black leather seats, the yellow light coming from the lamps on the tables and the ones hanging from the ceilings like a bunch of bells made this large space look cozy and welcoming.

The place was filling up. The band took their place, and the drinks were served as they started playing this cheerful music that made me feel like I accidentally walked into a party.

"Right," I sighed.

After a fleeting glance at Julie, who was talking to one of the witches, I made my way to the kitchen and closed the doors behind me, muffling the loud chitter and chatter. There were a few bottles of alcohol on the long wooden table. I grabbed a bottle of whiskey and one of the clean glasses sitting next to it and filled it up.

All I had this morning was a cup of coffee and one beignet, and as I took a large gulp from the glass, it burned my insides the whole way into my empty stomach. I grabbed a canape with salmon from the plate of finger food and sent it into my mouth. I leaned my back against the cabinet behind me while I chewed and watched the people in the bar through the glass doors.

There were nice words said about my father, about his devotion to our faction, his hard work to keep peace in this city, and about the tragic, untimely loss of their respected leader.

Words. Words.

"Close the door," I said as Simon walked in.

"Come on, Keira. You can't just hide here the whole night."

"Hide? You think I'm hiding?"

"Then why are you here?"

"I came here to avoid the false condolences."

"What makes you think they're false? People did respect him, you know."

"I've been watching them the whole day. There might be a couple who are truly sorry about what happened to Dad, and they all, or most of them, anyway, may have respected him when he was alive, but the second he's gone, no one cares about what happened, or why or who did it. I didn't hear anyone wonder who the hell could've killed him or talk about finding the killer and making him pay. Nothing." I scoffed. "All they talk about is me and who's going to be the next regent."

"Yeah." Simon heaved a breath. "I've heard some things too. But that's not a reason to sit here alone like a punished kid."

"Seriously?" I sneered. "I'm not the one punished. I'm waiting for the right moment—"

"Right moment for what? Keira, please." He shook his head. "This isn't the right time or place to attack people. It's Dad's funeral, for God's sake."

"I know that. That's why I didn't bring my gun and knife."

"You didn't bring them because, thanks to Julie, that dress doesn't have pockets."

I glanced through the glass door toward the stand where the photograph of my dad sat surrounded by candles. A guy in a black suit with his back to us added a single rose to the pile of flowers.

My eyes narrowed. "Is that Holden?"

"Yep. And at least one of us should be out there," Simon headed to the door, "to say things like, *hi,* and, *thank you,* you know."

"Well, you do that," I muttered under my breath watching him walk away and took another sip from my glass.

Simon approached Holden. After they exchanged a few words, Holden turned around and looked straight at me through the door.

My heart thumped a few extra beats. He hadn't changed much since the last time I saw him two years ago, and he was just as handsome.

We grew up together and went to the same school, and he always had a crush on me. We even dated a few times after we finished high school. But then I left. Without saying goodbye or leaving a note.

He never visited me in Atlanta, but a couple of years ago,

he found out from Simon that I was in Jacksonville for a few days and decided to meet me there.

That was the last time I saw him.

Holden walked into the room and closed the door. He didn't come closer and just looked at me from where he stood.

"Hi, Keira." He pushed back the sides of his blazer and slid his hands into his pockets.

"Hi." I straightened up.

"You're here. I'm glad you made it." He heaved a breath. "Though, I wish—"

"The circumstances were different." I finished the sentence for him.

"No." He frowned slightly. "I mean, that too. But I was going to say, I wish you'd come to see him when he was still alive."

"Seriously, Holden? I probably look like I'm not in enough pain, so you decided to fix it with your accusation?"

"I know you're in pain. I just wanted you to know that he missed you, and—"

"Gee, thanks. I feel much better." I took another gulp from my glass.

"And," Holden went on in the same calm tone, "that the day before his death, when the two of us were having a drink here, he said he was planning to visit you."

I stopped breathing. "What?"

After all those years?

My father never visited me. The last time I saw him was three years ago when I arrived in New Orleans at his request. He needed to open some family safe locked with my and Simon's blood. I stayed only a night. I left him a vial of my blood, but before leaving, I suggested it would be better if he changed the locks on that safe.

"Did he say why?"

"Yeah." Holden sighed. "He said your freedom will get

you in trouble and it's time to bring you home." I stared at him, and he continued, "To be honest, I was surprised too. I told him maybe it's a little late for that, that you're a grown-up, and if he couldn't convince you to come back before, what made him think he could do it now? He was always sure that you could take care of yourself, and I wondered what made him suddenly worry about you."

"Did you ask him?"

"I did. He said he had his reasons, though he didn't say what those reasons were."

Did Simon know anything about this? I didn't think he did. If he knew, he would've told me.

"How long are you staying?" Holden's brown eyes looked into mine.

"As long as it takes to find the killer. I imagine you're aware he didn't die from old age or a car crash."

"What's that supposed to mean? You think I don't care?"

I shrugged. "It seems no one gives a damn what happened."

"And you came to that conclusion after . . ." He spread his hands in frustration. "You just arrived."

"I've been watching them the whole day. Believe me, that was enough to—"

"To what? To think that you already know what's going on and lump me in as one of the crowd? I thought we knew each other better than that, Keira. Do you really think I would just let this go?"

"Holden." I shook my head. "I'm sorry. I'm just angry. I didn't mean to take it out on you. How about we start over?" I offered him a small smile. "Hi there. I'm glad to see you."

He rolled his eyes.

"What? I really am. How are you?" I put down my glass. "The last time we met, you said—"

The door behind him opened, and a young woman showed up on the threshold. "Holden, are you coming?"

Holden glanced back.

The woman gave me a sympathetic look. "Hi, Keira. I'm so sorry for—"

"She knows." Holden took her by the arm and led her away.

Well, that went smoothly. Does anyone ever finish their sentences here? And who the hell was that? Am I supposed to know her?

But that wasn't the question that bothered me. The sudden unpleasant feeling in my stomach was the result of not knowing who she was to Holden, and why she could so easily interrupt us and call him away.

But those thoughts were quickly eclipsed by other, more important ones.

Dad wanted to visit me. Why? Holden's words echoed in my mind: *He said your freedom will get you in trouble and it's time to bring you home.* Maybe I was in danger and he wanted to warn me? If that was so, then he probably wanted me back here so he could protect me. Could I be the reason he was killed?

Deciding I had collected enough information for one day to keep me up the whole night, I headed home.

CHAPTER 4

"Right," I sighed when I opened my eyes in the morning and remembered where I was.

For a second I felt warm and comfortable from this sudden wave of nostalgia. But then I remembered why I was here, and I closed my eyes again, wishing I was still asleep.

I groaned, lifting my heavy head from the pillow. It was an aftershock of yesterday's whiskey and my dismal thoughts, but I knew it wouldn't last long. Lately, I'd been healing fast. Not as fast as vampires or werewolves, but much faster than normal humans. Though I didn't know why. I thought it had something to do with my witch powers. Dad always said I wasn't like other witches, that I was much more powerful, and that he was sure I hadn't yet fully discerned my abilities. Maybe this was one of those abilities? But why now? I had a scar or two from before, but when I fell on broken glass a week ago and got deep cuts on my bare arms, they healed fast without leaving any marks.

After a quick shower, I walked out into the hallway and looked down at the courtyard. Simon was sitting in one of the armchairs around the small round table.

He looked up at me. "Morning."

"Hi." I glanced at the coffee cup in his hand. "Is there more?"

"Yeah. I just made it."

I chortled. "I didn't know you could do that. Where's Emily?" I asked, climbing down the stairs.

"She and Mike worked too hard these last few days. I gave them a day off."

"That's very thoughtful of you."

"I hope it's okay."

"Sure." I nodded. "I got used to doing things myself long ago."

"That's not what I meant. You're older than me. So you're the boss now. I just thought you could take a few days to look around before . . . you know?" He pursed his lips. "To catch up."

"That's fine. I'm not in a hurry to do any of those things." I wouldn't even know where to begin. "I trust you, little brother."

Simon smirked. "I'm flattered. And still, I would like you to repeat that after you've had your coffee."

I headed to the kitchen as I processed Simon's words. They made me realize how much everything has changed. Dad was the one giving orders in this house. With him gone, we were the responsible ones now. Thank God I'd learned how to pay bills and knew how to call a plumber if the pipes under my sink started leaking. But I had no idea how to keep order in this big house to ensure it didn't fall apart and look for my dad's killer at the same time.

I preferred to do the latter. That's what I was good at.

With the mug full of coffee, I returned to the courtyard and sank into the armchair across from Simon.

"I need to see the witches." I took a sip from my mug. "And I thought you could help me to gather them."

"Keira, did you hear what I just said? Maybe before

starting your interrogations, you should look around first. You've been gone awhile."

"Don't people say *strike while the iron is hot*? Besides, I know how to do my job."

"That's the thing. This isn't just another job to you. You're too invested in this one, and that's never a good sign. You're blinded by rage. That's why detectives are not allowed to investigate a crime that involves their relatives. Maybe it would be better if you spend a day," he put up his index finger, "one day, with someone you know well, someone close, like Julie."

Someone I know well.

"Simon, who was that girl with Holden? Is it his girlfriend?"

He heaved a breath. "Yeah. They've been dating a few months now."

"Hmm." My eyebrows slowly moved up. "Well, I hope he's happy. He deserves that."

"I wouldn't call them lovebirds, but they're doing okay." He observed me a moment, then asked, "Does it bother you?"

"No. Not really. But, you know." I shrugged. "It's a little unpleasant, like poking into an old wound with a blunt knife."

"I saw you two talking yesterday, and I kept her occupied for a bit so you could have some time alone. I'm sure you had a few things to talk about."

"Now that you mentioned that." I took another sip. "He said Dad was going to visit me in Atlanta. Did you know anything about it?"

"He did say he was planning to." Simon frowned. "He said things felt different lately."

"What things?"

"You. Something about you was different."

"Simon," I squinted, "I was hundreds of miles away. How could he know the difference?"

"Do you really think he would let you be out there all alone without him keeping an eye on you?" He rolled his eyes.

"What the hell are you saying? You don't mean I've been followed all those years, was I?"

"No. Not followed. But he had a protection spell around you. That's why he wanted to see you when he called you here three years ago. To renew the spell. It wasn't for your blood. He always had your blood in his stash."

I shook my head. "I can't believe this."

"What? You don't believe that he loved you so much that he couldn't be careless about you?"

"No. It's just, I'm not a kid anymore. Why would he worry so much?"

"I don't know." Simon spread his hands. "I asked him the same thing. He always said he had his reasons."

"So there's no safe locked with our blood, is there?"

"There is. But it's not locked with our blood. It's just yours, Keira."

"What's in it?" I stared at him.

He shrugged, resentment flashing in his eyes. "No idea."

After a moment of silence, I said, "I'm sorry, Simon."

"It's just . . ." He sighed. "I was here, with him, all this time. I did everything for him. But he still kept secrets from me. It hurts, you know. And," he jerked his shoulder, "he never worried about me like that."

I knew where his doubts were coming from. Simon wasn't my brother by blood. He was ten months old when he was adopted by my father.

My mom and Simon's parents died on the same day. They were killed by witches. Dad thought the killers were after Mom and that Simon's parents died trying to protect her.

I was only three then.

When I was old enough to know things, I asked Dad how Mom died and if he knew who the killers were. He told me that Mom died from stab wounds, but Simon's parents had no injuries. He assumed they were killed by a hex. That was why at first, he supposed the killers were witches.

However, over the years, he came up with new theories, but later on, he confessed that he wasn't sure if any of his theories were right.

He spent years trying to find out who the killers were and how exactly Simon's parents died. The whole faction helped. But they never found the truth. And whoever the killers were, they disappeared without a trace.

"Simon, listen to me." I put down my mug and leaned forward. "It doesn't mean he loved me more. Do you hear me? It only meant I was more dangerous. He worried about me because I was reckless. I have all these powers, and he thought that me living among normal people wasn't safe, that I could hurt someone."

"Did you?"

"No. I never hurt innocent people, only supernaturals. Though, once a woman got injured in the crossfire. Badly. She was in a hospital, and last I checked, she was still there. In a coma."

"Dammit, Keira." He stared at me. "Is there hope she'll ever wake up?"

"I don't think so. The doctors don't know what's wrong with her. She was knocked out by my magic, and I thought maybe I could help her. I snuck into the hospital a few times, tried to figure out what was wrong with her, but nothing I did helped. She didn't even blink."

"Maybe that's exactly what Dad was afraid of? It's not you who's dangerous, Keira. It's your magic."

"Yeah, I suppose so. And it's not that I can't control it. He took so much time to teach me, and I was doing pretty well. I just don't fully understand my powers yet. And that woman," I shrugged, "she saw no danger when she jumped in the middle. People can't see magic, which means they don't see the danger. But they can see a gun. After that accident, I started using weapons to be on the safe side, and I only use my magic for small things."

Simon's eyes fixed on the cap in his hand.

"Simon, Dad always said he had his reasons to worry. I want to open the safe. Maybe what he kept inside will help me understand what those reasons were."

"I was thinking the same."

"You know where it is, don't you?"

"It's in his study." He put the cap down and got to his feet. "Come on."

My heart squeezed as I walked into my father's study—a room I hadn't set foot in since I drove away three years ago without saying goodbye.

Simon rounded the old mahogany desk and pulled aside the chair.

"He kept the safe in his desk?"

"It's not like a safe safe, it's . . ." He bent down and pulled out the bottom drawer on the left side. "Come here." He stepped aside.

I approached the desk and looked into the drawer. "Simon, there's nothing there."

"Not yet." He smiled. "Touch it."

I crouched before the desk and lowered my hand into the drawer. It didn't go in, but hit a hard invisible surface.

"Do you feel anything?"

"It's warm."

"Only warm? When I touched it, it almost burned my hand. When I first looked inside and didn't see anything, I thought whatever was in it was probably deeper in the drawer. I thrust my hand in and nearly broke my fingers."

"Come on," I chuckled. "You knew it was enchanted. Nosy much?"

Simon laughed. "I know. One day my curiosity will get me into serious trouble."

"I bet you even stole some of my blood from Dad's stash to open it."

"You really think he would just leave it lying around? That was locked with a spell too."

I chuckled again. "I feel for you."

"It was a few years ago. I was still young and stupid."

I sighed, remembering the last time I was here. "After I gave him my blood, I left early in the morning when you two were still asleep. I snuck out so I wouldn't have to say goodbye."

"That was mean. Don't you ever do that again."

"I won't. I promise."

Once again, the guilt surged through me. If I'd only known I would never see my dad again, that it was my only chance to say goodbye to him before he died.

Simon opened a drawer on the right side of the desk, pulled out a small dagger, and handed it over.

"And this." From the same drawer, he pulled out a patch and dropped it on the chair next to me. "For your wound. Well, you know what to do, sis." He headed for the door. "I'll leave you to it. God," he glanced back, smirking. "I hope it's not just cash and a textbook to teach witches how to not put people in a coma."

He closed the door behind him, and I sat on the floor before the drawer. I winced as I drove the sharp blade over my palm. The moment the blood pooled from the cut, I squeezed my hand into the fist. Holding it above the hard surface of the drawer, I dripped four drops of my blood as if I were marking the points of an invisible cross. When I dripped the last drop into the center, red lines came out from all four points and dashed to the middle. The moment the blood-cross was complete, the wooden lid became visible.

The blood on my cut was already clotting, but I patched

the wound anyway. Simon knew nothing about my healing abilities, and I didn't want him to ask questions I had no answers for.

I drove the tip of the dagger into the slit between the lid and the side of the drawer, put a little pressure on the hilt, and the lid popped up.

The first thing I saw when I removed the lid was a hairbrush. It was my mom's. Even though I was only three when she died, I recognized it at once. My throat tightened. As I picked up the hairbrush, my mom looked at me from the photograph beneath, holding a little me in her arms. I swallowed the lump in my throat. I hadn't seen this picture since I ran away ten years ago.

The next item in the drawer was an envelope. I put the hairbrush and the photograph on the desk and picked it up. Beneath it, at the bottom of the drawer, lay my bank card. My lips twitched in a smile as I remembered Simon's words. I took the card and pushed it into my pocket.

There was something heavy in the envelope. I looked inside and saw a big, old-fashioned, and slightly rusty key. I tilted the envelope and dropped it into my hand. *What's this for?*

Feeling nervous, I pulled out the letter. I identified my dad's handwriting at once.

My dear Keira,

I was planning to visit you. This note was only an extra precaution. But if you're reading this, it means I'm gone, and most definitely I didn't die from natural causes. If that's so, then it also means you're in danger.

I know you'll do anything to find the killer, but you won't find whoever did it among our witches or the members of other factions of our city. The cause of this crime goes way back and is much more complicated.

You always wondered what happened to your mother, and I bet you still have questions about your powers, which I know for sure you haven't fully mastered.

Your mother, my beloved wife Esther, was not an ordinary witch, Keira. I always suspected that she had another, much more powerful kind of blood running through her veins, and I'm sure that was the reason she was hunted.

I don't know who was after her. All she told me was that she'd done something to someone very powerful, that he would not rest until he made her pay, and that the less I knew, the safer I would be. Maybe if I'd had more time with her, she would have opened up eventually. But, as you know, our time together was cut short.

I don't know to this day what happened. All I know is that she was attacked in an alley, and by the time I got there, Simon's parents and Esther lay dead on the ground. Esther died from injuries, but Simon's parents had no wounds. I assumed they were killed by powerful magic, but I didn't get a chance to examine their bodies.

I supposed whoever was hunting Esther had finally found her.

You're her daughter, and she always feared that if they found out about you, you'd be in as much danger. That's why, in case something happened to her, your mother taught me the complicated protection spell she cast around you the day you were born, and which I've been renewing every five years.

But about a week ago, that spell was broken. It means something has changed. I have no clue what caused the change, and I wanted to find out so I could protect you.

Apparently, I was on the right track and it didn't end well. So it seems you're on your own now.

I know you were never much of a people-person and you like to do things yourself, but still, I'm so sorry for leaving you alone with all these questions.

I always knew there was much more to the story than the one Esther shared with me. And it was much more complicated and dangerous. I believed it even more when a couple of months after her death, I found in one of her drawers a few pieces of golden metal that looked like part of a broken object.

I examined those pieces and found them extremely powerful. However, their energy was alien to me. Unfortunately, I couldn't discover more. But I think you can. And you should. It will help you learn what are you up against.

Before she met me, your mother lived in Pennsylvania, in a small town called Whispering Pines. She had a house there. She was very fond of it, and she hoped to show it to you one day. I think that's where you should go to find the answers.

Goodbye, my strong, brave Keira.

Your loving dad.

"DON'T WORRY, DAD, I'LL GET TO THE BOTTOM OF THIS. I promise." I brushed off the single tear that skipped my eye as I blinked.

I glanced at the back of the paper. There was the address and my mom's name. Esther Millweard. *Millweard?* I never knew my mom's maiden name.

I ran my hand deeper into the drawer and found what I was looking for. A rectangular wooden box. The box wasn't locked, and when I lifted the lid, I saw three pieces of gold that had an interesting form. They were oblong, slightly convex, and pointy, like big claws, or like talons. I picked one up. It was warm. Its energy felt familiar, and the moment I locked my fingers around it, I felt like it belonged to me. Which only proved that it belonged to my mother.

It was my fault Dad was dead. All my fault. All this time he made me think that I was the dangerous one. But it was me who was in danger, and he was only trying to protect me. Whoever killed him wasn't after him. They were after me.

I got to my feet. I had to leave. Immediately. My being here put Simon in danger too, and I could never forgive myself if something happened to him.

I headed to my room wondering how much of what I just learned I could tell Simon. Composing our conversation, I mentally went through Dad's letter. I scratched off sentence after sentence until I was left with only a few lines.

I was locking my suitcase when Simon showed up in the doorway.

"What are you doing?" He looked shocked and angry at the same time. "Keira, what's going on?"

"I'm sorry, Simon, but I have to leave." I pursed my lips. "Again."

"Why?" He stared at me. "I thought you wanted to find Dad's killer. What changed? Is it because of what you found in that drawer?"

"Yes. Dad never got over Mom's death, and he was still searching for answers. He also knew it was dangerous and if something happened to him, I'd start looking for his killers, but he is . . . was sure that whoever they are, they aren't from New Orleans. Not our witches or anybody from the other factions are responsible for his death. But he left me some hints, and that's where I'm going. I have to check them out."

"I should come with you."

"No. You should take care of this place. If you come with me, all I'll be thinking about is keeping you safe."

"Do I look helpless to you?" He raised his hand and squeezed it into a fist, and the whole room shook.

"No. Come on, that's not what I mean. I know how powerful you are. But the fear that you could get hurt will keep me on my toes. And," I raised my finger, "you said it yourself: I'm older and I'm the boss. What I say goes. And it's not just me." I had to improvise to make him forget about following me. "Dad said he was sure you would keep our home safe. Don't worry, little brother, I'll find them."

"Oh, that's exactly what I'm worried about. They are not amateurs, Keira. They managed to kill Dad."

"I'm sure it only happened because there were too many

of them and they ambushed him. And whoever they are, they don't know I exist. That's what he needed my blood for. He used it to keep me cloaked. There is a difference between someone looking for you and you being the one to do the looking. He was the hunted. But me? I'm the hunter. It's what I do."

Simon heaved a breath and pushed his hands into his pockets. "Was there anything else?"

"Yep." I grinned. "My bank card."

He chortled. "I'm glad you got your money back. There's also his will, of course—"

"Simon, it's not important right now."

"True. But I just wanted to let you know that—"

"I know, and I trust you to take care of it, okay?"

He gave me a warm smile, and I felt the urge to say it to him, the words I never got to say to my mom or my dad. "I love you, Simon." I drew closer and locked my arms around his neck. "You're all I've got. So please, take care of yourself."

He hugged me back. "I love you too, sis."

"Listen." I let go of him. "How about a lunch at the bar with Julie and Holden before I leave? I don't want to disappear like before, without goodbyes. Holden wanted to help me find Dad's killer, so I'll tell him I'm off to follow a lead and he doesn't need to worry about it. I don't want him involved in any of this. He should stay with his girl."

"Yeah." He nodded. "I'll make the calls. They'll love that."

CHAPTER 5

The sun was still up when I arrived in Whispering Pines the next day. I stopped at a small store to buy something to eat for the next morning, and coffee, hoping there would be a coffee maker. I had no idea what the house looked like, and since no one had lived in it for more than two decades, I didn't expect it to have a functioning fridge or even electricity. But I hoped there was an intact roof and a bed I could crash on tonight. I'd figure out the rest tomorrow.

Behind the cash register stood a tall, curvy woman around sixty with curled red hair. When I loaded the groceries on the counter, her brow arched slightly as she looked at me.

"Hello," she said, which sounded more like a question.

"Hi." I raised both of my brows in reply.

"Sorry." She smiled. "I'm trying to figure out . . . Are you Lucy's niece?"

"No." I returned the smile. "I'm no one's niece."

As I paid, she took a paper bag from the stack next to the cashier and opened it. "Oh, so just passing by then?"

"Actually, I'm planning to stay for a while."

"Stay? That's nice. We all love to see fresh faces here."

Without taking her eyes off me, she slowly shifted the groceries into the bag. "Stay where?"

It was obvious that she wouldn't let me go until I satisfied her curiosity. Luckily, I came up with a story on my way here in case there were nosy neighbors nearby the house.

"I rented that house in Silent Woods. I'm a writer, and I needed a quiet place to work," I said, hoping my answer contained enough information to end this unexpected interview.

"The Lily House?" Her hand holding the box of eggs froze in the air. When I looked at her, perplexed, she added, "I mean, the Millweard's place?"

Millweard's place? Is that what they call Mom's house here after all these years?

"Yeah," I nodded. I shifted from foot to foot, becoming more and more uncomfortable with this conversation. "That one."

She resumed the packing. "He rented it out? He's never done that before."

He? Who was the *he*? Was she talking about Dad?

"But now that I think about it, who would ever want to stay at that creepy . . ." The woman cleared her throat. "I mean, that place could use a woman's touch." She threw a fleeting glance at the ketchup stain on my shirt.

I rubbed it with my middle finger. "Yeah, it's probably not a good idea to eat while driving."

"Here you go." She finally handed me my groceries.

"Thanks." I grabbed the bag and headed for the exit.

"What did you say your name was?"

"I didn't."

"Good luck with your writing," she threw after me, and right before the door closed, I heard her suppressed chuckle.

"Great!" I muttered under my breath.

The population of Whispering Pines barely reached two and a half thousand people—I looked it up on the way—and

I never stayed in small places like this. In Atlanta, most people had no clue who lived next door, when in this town it would be impossible to stay unnoticed and left alone. It seemed not only a big challenge for someone like me, but also very inconvenient, considering the fact that my identity was supposed to be a secret. But on the other hand, those talkative people who knew everything about everyone could help me find the answers I was looking for.

I kept driving by the river, following the GPS instructions, and after a couple of minutes, it led me into the woods.

The rays of the setting sun shot through the lush branches arched above the road, sending shadows of leaves running up the windshield. Taking in the surrounding beauty, I opened the window and inhaled blown-in from the depths of the woods the delicate scent of pines.

A few moments later, I saw wide-open wooden gates at the end of the road. My jaw dropped as I drove through them into the big yard.

"You gotta be kidding me," I replied to the GPS when it announced, "You've reached your destination."

What I was looking at wasn't some small, derelict house. This place still looked a little neglected, but it was a two-and-a-half-story eighteenth-, or maybe even seventeenth-, century manor.

My gaze traveled to the woods surrounding the yard. "No nosy neighbors, then," I noted with delight.

I came out of the car, approached the wide, long porch with wooden pillars, and stopped before the tall oak double doors. When I looked up, I saw an image of a water lily imprinted on the bar above.

Still doubting that I was in the right place, I pulled the key out of my bag. It would be funny if I were trying to unlock someone else's door. They would probably freak out, especially if they were, for some reason, walking around naked.

Maybe I should knock first?

I did. But nothing happened.

It was getting dark, I was tired, and I didn't have the slightest desire to drive around without a clue what I was looking for. I decided to trust my GPS.

"Let's see," I muttered, sticking the key into the rusty lock. I turned it and heard the clack.

"Hallelujah!" I breathed out with relief and pushed the door open.

I walked in and found myself standing in the middle of a foyer big enough to fit my whole apartment in Atlanta. Across from me, a wide, oak staircase with a polished banister ran up to a second-floor landing designed as a balcony. Through the rectangular hole between the balcony railings, I could see a part of the carved wooden ceiling. But I couldn't see the details of the pattern clearly. The ceiling was high, and it was getting dark.

The patterned floor was a little dusty, and there were some spider webs in the corners here and there, but all together, the place looked tidy.

A glanced at the chandelier hanging from the foyer ceiling. Before closing the door and cutting myself off from the only source of the light coming from outside, I looked around for a switch. I found it on the wall next to the front door. Crossing my fingers on one hand, I flipped the switch with the other.

"Yes!" My jubilant whisper rang out as the warm yellow light filled the hall. It did seem strange that this abandoned place still had electricity, but I decided I was just that lucky.

Counting on that same luck, I hoped this place had running water. I closed the front door and glanced first at the room through the wide archway on my left and then through the one on my right, looking for the kitchen.

"Who the hell are you?" a pissed-off female voice said.

I spun around and looked at the stairs.

What I was looking at wasn't human. At least, not a living one.

"You are a ghost." I pointed at her as she sat on the round stand at the bottom of the stairs.

"You don't say. And all this time I thought I was just a fluffy cloud." She got up and put her hands on her waist as she floated above the stairs.

She was a plump woman around fifty, wearing a knee-length, light floral dress that danced around her as she wiggled her hips from side to side.

I smiled.

"What are you smiling about? You should be running away screaming, like every other normal human."

So that's what that lady from the store meant when she called this place creepy. The house was haunted.

"I'm not afraid of you. But I'm a little surprised. How can I see you? I've never seen ghosts before."

"Interesting question. I'm surprised too. People can't hear me, and they don't usually see me. Well, at least the normal ones."

"I thought ghosts couldn't talk."

"Oh dear, I can do more than that," she giggled. She flew to the switch, and the next moment, I was standing in darkness.

"That's not funny," I said as she cackled next to my ear. "I already told you, I'm not afraid of you." I pulled out my phone and lit my way to the switch.

She was nowhere to be seen, but the moment I turned on the lights, she turned them off again.

"I understand," I sighed. "You've been here alone all this time, you're bored and you want to play, but can we do this some other time? I had a very long ride, and I'm pretty tired."

Her laughter rang out all around me.

"I said, turn the lights on," I said through gritted teeth. "Now."

Silence fell at once, and the lights came on.

"Thank you," I barked.

"Thank me?" She appeared in front of me, her expression puzzled. "What the hell just happened?"

Frowning, I tilted my head. "What do you mean?"

"I mean, you forced me to do it. I wasn't going to turn on the lights, but I did it anyway."

"Listen, I swear I'll play along tom—"

"Oh my! You're *her,* aren't you?"

"*Her? Her* who?"

"He warned me you might show up!"

"Who?" But before she could answer, I raised my finger again. "Wait, so are you saying I can force you to do things?"

She thrust her fists into her sides. "You can't abuse that power. Good people don't force others to do their bidding. They ask. Politely."

"All right. Could you shut up for a second, *please*?" I looked around. "Which way is the kitchen?"

Her fists still on her waist, she nodded to my left. "Just go through the great room."

The furniture in the great room was covered with white sheets. I turned on the lamp on the small round table, threw a glance at the paintings on the walls, and continued to the open door at the end of the room.

The lights went on the moment I walked into the kitchen. I glanced back over my shoulder and saw the ghost hovering in the doorway

"What's your name?"

"Penny," she said, and as she beamed, I supposed no one had asked her that question for a very long time.

"Thanks, Penny."

The kitchen was huge. Closer to the door, there was a long wooden table with eight simple wooden chairs. Behind the table was a square marble island with drawers, and behind the island, there was a big stove with six burners.

Suddenly I wished I could cook.

A window above the sink looked out at the right side of the yard, and the rest of the wall was covered in shelves and cabinets. I approached the sink and opened the tap. The faucet coughed a few times, then spat out a few brown drops right before the same color water burst out of it.

I heaved a breath. "Glad I have a bottle of water in the car."

"Oh, don't worry," Penny, who seemed in a much better mood now, rushed to my side. "It'll get better. Just let it run for a few minutes."

I crossed to the fridge beside more cabinets on the other side of the room. "What about this?" I pulled open the door. The fridge was dark and empty.

"It works. It's just unplugged."

I plugged it in, and the light inside the fridge came on. "That's a miracle." At this, Penny giggled again. "No, I mean it. How come everything is working when no one has been living here?"

"He doesn't live here, but he shows up from time to time, you know. He hasn't been here for a while, so I'm sure he'll come check on the place soon."

She must've meant Dad, and I didn't want to tell her he'd never come back. She was alone all the time and probably fond of the only human visiting this place. It seemed that my appearance brightened her lone existence, and I didn't want to traumatize her just yet.

I'll tell her later.

"What's there?" I asked, pointing at the door next to the fridge.

"The utility rooms. The storage, the laundry room, a bathroom. And if you walk through that passage, you'll come out at the dining room, then the study, and then the hall again. Do you want me to show you? I could give you a full tour."

She seemed pretty excited, and I did want to check out

this amazing house, but not right now. Right now all I wanted was to eat something and get some sleep.

"How about we do that tomorrow? But I would like you to show me the bedroom with the most comfortable bed. I'll get my things from the car."

"You need a hand? I can lift things if they're not too heavy."

"You can leave the house?"

"Yeah, but not the property," she said grumpily. "I'm pinned to this place."

I walked back to the sink. "You were right. The water is much cleaner now."

"This one." Penny pointed at one of the doors on the second floor. "This is the master bedroom, and it's big and cozy. The bed looks good too, but I never slept in it, so I don't know for sure. It might be a bit dusty, though."

"I'm a bit dusty myself at the moment, so we're a perfect match."

"And the room looks at the front yard," she went on. "I figure this might be important, you know, having a view of your yard if you're staying alone."

"Why? Do you get many onlookers or intruders here?"

"No." she shook her head. "Only some stupid kids, and mostly at Halloween. Sometimes I make it fun for them, and sometimes I scare the hell out of them. Depends on my mood."

I glanced around while she talked, eyeing the faded sage-green wallpaper with pale pink flowers, the fireplace under the wall across from the bed, the chest of drawers with a lamp on top, then turned my eyes back to the big bed with a carved, polished wooden headboard.

The air in the room was warm and stale. I pulled aside the

light curtains and opened the window, letting in the fresh breeze.

"But now that you're here, who knows?" Penny continued. "Maybe the grownups will get curious and come check on the woman who's brave enough to stay in this abandoned haunted house. You are going to stay here, aren't you? Ah, what did you say your name was? Wait, you never did."

"I'm Keira, and yes, I will. Just don't know for how long yet." I removed the cover from the bed, and as I threw it on the armchair, a cloud of dust shot up in the air.

"There are more covers here." Penny flew to the chest of drawers and returned holding a blanket. "This one's good." She handed it over.

I turned on the lamp on the nightstand, turned off the ones on the wall, and took off my pants.

"That's a nasty cut you got there."

She referenced the scar on my back. I pulled down the edge of my tank top to cover it and dived under the blanket. "It was just a scratch."

"It was a pretty deep one, if you ask me."

"I didn't." Her excited rambling was getting to me. I closed my eyes, hoping she'd get the hint and disappear.

"How did you get it?"

"It's a work injury," I yawned.

"Must be a very dangerous job. What do you do?"

"I'm a writer."

"A writer? But . . ." She first stared at me, then smirked. "A writer, huh? What do you write about?"

"Pennyyyy," I growled. "Don't make me—"

"Okay, okay." She giggled quietly. "Welcome to Lily House," she whispered.

The nightstand light went off, and she was gone.

CHAPTER 6

"Coffee is ready," a cheerful voice said.

I opened my eyes.

It took me a moment to remember where I was and why there was a ghost hovering at the foot of my bed. I blinked a few times, then sat up and leaned against the headboard.

"Penny," I croaked, "we need to set house rules. Rule one, my bedroom is my personal space and you're not allowed here without permission. Got it?"

"I just wanted to let you know—"

"Do you get it?" I asked again.

The corners of her mouth slid down. She nodded, turned around, and flew out through the wall.

I knew she meant well, but all this talking before sleep when it was usually *me* time and waking up from someone talking to me when I was still asleep was too annoying. I wasn't used to it. I never lived with a man because I never had a long-term relationship, and I never had a roommate, especially someone my mom's age. And I hadn't had a mom since I was three, to begin with.

I sighed. Her sad face made me feel evil.

"Penny?" I called quietly.

"Yes?" She popped up in the room, beaming.

"Nothing." I couldn't suppress the smile. "I was only wondering if this house is soundproofed. Apparently, it isn't."

"Well," she pursed her lips guiltily, "I was right behind the door."

"Go. I'll be downstairs in a minute."

As she left the room, I got up and opened my suitcase. The box with the golden pieces—in my head I called them talons—was wrapped in one of my T-shirts. I unwrapped it, got up, and went back to the nightstand. The drawer was empty, as I expected. I put the box inside, then forced my magic into my palm and, holding it above the box, muttered, "Obscure." The box became invisible. This spell wasn't as strong as my father's, but it would do for now.

Penny, who was looking out the window, turned around the moment I walked into the kitchen.

"Aren't you going to eat something?" she asked as I poured myself a cup of coffee and sat at the table.

"First I need to take a shower."

"I already ran the water clean for you in the second-floor bathroom. It's the one next to your bedroom."

"You did?"

"Yes." She grinned. "The night is long, and it was nice to have something to do while waiting for you to wake up. I also dusted a little and removed most of the cobwebs. I've done housework around here before. The things I can manage. But I do it rarely, out of boredom, and it's so much nicer to do it for someone."

It was her domain and, as far as I knew, ghosts were extremely protective of their territory. It seemed strange that Penny didn't mind sharing the house with someone she knew nothing about. But then, it seemed she was a people-person, and to be cut off from society for who knows how long must've been torture for someone like Penny.

"Keira," she landed behind the table, "how did you end up here?"

"Actually, that would be my question." I sipped from the cup. "You said you're pinned to this house. Why? Did you die here?"

"No. I died in town. In my house."

"Then what are you doing here?"

"I owed a favor to someone, and I'm paying it off. I'm here to look after this place."

Was she talking about my mom? "Who did you owe a favor?"

"Sorry, I can't tell you. That's part of the deal."

"Okay. Then can you tell me when you died?"

"Twenty-seven years ago."

"Did you know the owner of this house?"

"I did. But she left this place long ago. It's been about twenty-six years since last I saw her."

"And how long have you been here?"

"Almost as long. But she wasn't the one I made the deal with, if that's where you're going."

Right. Yesterday she said, *He warned me you might show up,* so it wasn't a woman.

I sighed. "Yesterday you said, 'You're her, aren't you?' What did you mean by that?"

"I was told that someone might show up. A woman. So I thought you were her."

"Who told you that?"

"The same one I can't talk about."

"God, I hope it's not Voldemort." I rolled my eyes.

"Who's that?"

"Never mind." She was locked up here for more than a quarter of the century, and I wasn't surprised she didn't understand my reference. "What else did he say about me?"

"About you? So I was right, then. You *are* her. And that's why you have power over me. Because you're not an ordinary human."

I was back to my first guess and was now ninety-nine percent sure she was talking about Dad. He knew one day I would come here. He probably has done something for Penny while she was alive, and in return, he asked her to protect the house until I showed up.

But it was the one percent that bothered me. Why would he hide his name?

"Yes, I'm *her*. Which means you don't need to hide his identity from me anymore. Was his name—" Penny stuck her transparent fingers into her transparent ears and flew out of the window before I said, "—Josef Hale?"

After the shower, I wrapped myself in the towel and went to the bedroom to put some fresh clothes on. It was only nine in the morning, but the air was already hot, so I picked a tank top and a pair of shorts. I put them on, then closed the suitcase and dragging it after me, headed to the wardrobe. The moment I pulled open the doors, I froze to the spot.

When I was driving here, I was thinking about this house as something that belonged to my mom, but the moment I arrived, I somehow associated it with my dad. Penny's appearance was a distraction, and I was too tired to pay much attention to details.

Now, my feelings stirred up, putting me into an emotional stupor as I stood staring at a couple of dresses and a few blouses on the hangers. Were these my mother's clothes? I was sure that she took everything with her when she moved to New Orleans, and since no one lived here after that, this place should be empty.

Maybe it was the clothes she didn't like, or perhaps she left them here so she wouldn't have to carry much when she decided to visit this place. But even then, why would her clothes still be here after all this time?

Maybe they weren't hers. There were several other bedrooms in this house, and any of them could've been Mom's.

But then I remembered that Penny said this one was the biggest. The master bedroom.

"This was my mom's," I murmured under my breath, my eyes still fixed on the clothes.

"Your mom's?" Penny gasped next to me. "Oh my God, you're Esther Millweard's daughter."

I was so deep in my thoughts that I forgot to be angry with her for appearing here without permission.

"They're hers, aren't they?" I asked to make sure no one else lived here after her death.

"They're hers. No one ever stayed in this bedroom but her. Not even in the house. Well, except *him,* of course." Penny's voice became smaller. "You didn't know because . . . she died, didn't she?"

I nodded.

"When?"

"I was three."

"I'm so sorry, Keira. I'll let you have a moment." With a sigh, she drifted away.

I pulled out one of the blouses, put it to my chest, and ran my hand over its soft fabric. Then I pulled out another hanger and looked at the cocktail dress hanging on it.

Are there places here where she could wear this? I tried to imagine it on Mom. But the few memories I had of her had faded away, and to see her clearly, I had to look at her picture.

I hung the dress back and turned to the chest of drawers. After I checked it out and found it empty, I pulled my suitcase closer and started unpacking.

I RETURNED TO THE KITCHEN, OPENED THE FRIDGE, AND PULLED out everything I needed for a sandwich. While making it, I tried to figure out my next step.

Dad said I was in danger. That meant the person who killed both my parents was now after me. To find out who they were, I needed to learn more about Mom, about the time she lived here.

Where do I start?

"Penny?"

She appeared in front of me. "Yes?"

I put the sandwich on the plate and sat at the table. "You said you knew my mother?"

"I did, yes. The whole town knew her. She was about your age when I died." She sighed. "I liked her a lot. We all did. And I'm not saying it because you're her daughter. I'm saying this because it's true."

"Tell me something about her."

"She was kind. She helped people with their problems."

"What kind of problems?"

"You see," she cleared her throat, "this town isn't like any other. Things happened here. But she knew how to deal with those things. We all suspected that she was . . . How do I put it. . . ?"

I gave her a look. "Just say it."

She clasped her hands behind her back. "Different."

I nodded my eyes at my plate. "Penny, no one can know who I am. Not yet," I said with a warning in my voice.

"Okay. Besides," she shrugged, "who's gonna ask me? And you do remember that no one can see or hear me, right?"

I gave her a sideways look. The fact that I could see a ghost and talk to it seemed so normal to me now that I kept forgetting others couldn't.

And that was the reason she was so happy to have me here.

"Right. But it's like you said, things are different now. I wouldn't be surprised if someone *different*, like me, suddenly pops up on our doorstep." I took a bite from my sandwich.

After I finished eating, Penny showed me the rest of the house. I tried to be patient while she told me how she dusted off the books and the artwork, but when she started describing in detail how she managed to get the dust from under the sofas and every corner of the house, I cut the tour short.

"Thanks, Penny," I said the moment she finished the first floor.

I stepped outside.

My eyes traveled around as I stood on the porch listening to the silence. It was too quiet. It would take time for me to get used to it after living in a big, noisy city like Atlanta.

I knew she was right behind me. "Why is the house called Lily?" I asked, walking down the porch stairs.

"Come with me. I'll show you."

Soaring a few feet above the ground, Penny rounded the house and led me to the backyard. We walked down the green court surrounded by tall pines and came out to a pond shoreline.

The pond had an oval shape. It was about forty feet long and thirty feet wide. Its calm surface was covered in white and peach water lilies and surrounded by tall grass and colorful wildflowers.

The warm feelings this mesmerizing view raised inside me brought a smile to my face. But at the same time, it awakened a nervous fluttering in my stomach. The pond felt familiar to me, and the inexplicable sense of connection to it could only come from the fact that this place had belonged to my mother.

Which meant that now, it belonged to me.

"Penny, you said my mother helped people. Do you

remember who those people were? I'd like to hear their stories."

"Let me see." She scratched her temple. "She helped Ervin. And I remember she helped Laura, though I don't know exactly what the problem was. Dolly's story was interesting. When I say interesting . . . I mean . . . it didn't end well for her husband. There were also Martin and Cassie, but they moved shortly after the accident."

CHAPTER 7

I decided to visit Ervin first. I got in the car and headed to town. Following Penny's instructions, I found the right street and the house with the right number on a small, rusty plate.

Eying the overgrown bushes in the front yard, I approached the small wooden gate and pushed it open. The shabby stairs squeaked under my feet as I climbed to the porch. Despite the heat, the windows were closed and the curtains were shut, and all together, the place looked deserted.

Penny said that back then, Ervin was around fifty. Hoping the old man liked a quiet life and was chilling in his back-yard, I knocked on the door.

But my positivity didn't pay off, and I went to the house across the road.

The young woman who answered the door smiled at me. "Hello. How can I help you?"

"Hi. I was wondering if someone lives in that house." I pointed my thumb behind my back.

"No. Not for a while. Are you looking for someone in particular?"

"I was hoping to see Ervin Miller."

"Ervin?" The woman's eyebrows jumped up. "I'm sorry, but Ervin died fifteen years ago. His kids moved away a few years after that, but if you're a relative—"

"Oh, no," I waved my hand dismissively.

"You must be . . . are you the young lady staying at Lily House?"

And it's not even noon yet.

"That's me."

She opened her mouth to ask her next question, but I decided to close it for her. With the words, "Sorry for bothering you," I turned around and walked away.

My next stop was Laura. Penny said she was younger than Ervin, and I hoped she was still alive.

And she was. But she'd been locked up in a mental health center for the last seventeen years.

Luckily, Dolly Benson was still alive and sane. And she was happy to talk to the *brave woman,* as she called me, who was staying in the creepy, haunted manor.

She invited me inside, and as I sat on the couch, she said, "It's hot outside. I'll get us something cold to drink," and rushed to the kitchen.

I looked around while I waited. There were colorful flowers in pots on the windowsills, and on the dresser, there was a framed picture of the much younger Dolly with a man who was probably her husband. The furniture had seen better days, but it was well taken care of.

"So what is it you wanted to talk to me about, my dear?" She put two glasses of iced tea on the coffee table, one for each of us, and sat across from me in the stuffed armchair.

"I wanted to ask you about Esther Millweard. I've heard she helped you once."

"About Esther?" She blinked a few times. "Are you related to her? You said your name was Keira . . ."

"Keira Hale. And no. I'm a writer, and I'm interested in

the history of this town. I've heard strange accidents happened here and Esther helped the people involved."

"An accident is a car crash, or if you slip on ice and break your leg. What Esther was helping with . . . " Dolly shook her head. "Those were no accidents, my dear. Those were bizarre, mysterious events."

"I've heard she helped you once. Was your story bizarre and mysterious too?"

"It was, and I'm afraid you'll think I'm crazy if I told you the true story."

"You can't surprise me, Mrs. Benson. I'm a fantasy writer."

"My dear, if you keep calling me Mrs. Benson, I'll feel like I'm talking to a policeman who's writing up a police report. Call me Dolly, it's friendlier."

I looked at the sweet, gray-haired woman in front of me and nodded. "Dolly, could you please tell me what happened to your husband all those years ago?"

She was right, I did sound like a policeman. Writer, my ass. But in my defense, I worked with monsters. I didn't need to make friendly conversation with them to put a bullet in their heads.

"It's been a long time since I talked about it, especially after Peter died." She leaned back. "It happened twenty-nine years ago. Our son was only eleven. That night, he was on his bike, driving home from his friend's house. He burst in all terrified, shut the door, and said he was chased by a wolf. Peter thought Tony was overreacting. He said there are no wolves in Pennsylvania and it must have been someone's dog. But then we heard a growl. Peter looked out the window, then without a word, he grabbed his rifle from the hallway closet and stormed out. I told Tony to stay inside and ran after him.

"He shot the wolf. He didn't have a choice. It was huge and it came at Peter. But then," Dolly leaned forward again and locked her hands in her lap. "Right in front of our eyes, the wolf turned into a human. A young man. I still remember the tattoo of a growling wolf on his forearm." She heaved a breath. "We couldn't believe our eyes. Peter kept saying, 'It was a wolf, it was a wolf, I would never . . . I would never.'

"We stood staring at the naked man lying in front of us, both petrified. Then Peter said we had to remove the body before Tony saw it. While I made sure Tony was nowhere around, Peter drove his car close to the man and put him in the trunk. Then the two of us drove right to Esther. We knew we wouldn't be the first ones to ask her for help. Why? Because she was a problem-solver. And because she believed people no matter how crazy their stories sounded. Nothing seemed to faze her. It was like she knew something we didn't."

"And did she help?" I asked.

"She did. She said she believed us and knew Peter would never shoot a human being. She said not to worry, that she'd take care of it, and she took the body from us. A week later, right before Esther left Whispering Pines, Peter was found dead in the woods with lacerated wounds and bite marks. They said it was an animal attack."

"Dolly, that night when Peter shot the man, were you sure he was dead?"

"I was then. But here's the thing. Not even a week ago, when I was on my way home from Barbara's house—an old friend of mine—I swear I saw him walking down the street right before he turned onto Dark Alley. Dark Alley is a shady place, and I don't usually drive that way, but there was a problem with the main road, and it was closed that night. I know it's been a long time, but I could never forget his face. And what's even more disturbing, he looked just the same. Not a day older than the night Peter shot him.

"I wished Esther was still here so I could ask if it was possible the man was still alive. What if he survived? What if he was the one who killed Peter? But she's gone. She moved somewhere south, and we haven't seen her since. That's strange too. She loved her Lily House, and I hoped one day she'd come visit, at least for a few days, to check on it. But she never did. I've heard the house is being taken care of by someone else."

I swallowed the lump in my throat. I didn't want her to think that Mom just abandoned them all and left them unprotected.

"Before coming here, I did some research on Esther Millweard. She did love her house, and she didn't come back because she died a few years after she moved from Whispering Pines."

"Oh, no," Dolly gasped. "She was still so young and I never thought . . . Do you know what happened? Was there an accident? Did she get sick?"

Oooh, Dolly, I'm afraid you will have to keep guessing.

"Sorry, but I didn't find anything about the cause of her death."

I took a sip of my iced tea.

She did too before she spoke again. "She was good for this town. She understood people. And she dealt with the mysterious things happening here which we didn't want to believe were real. Well." She took another sip and put her glass down. "I hope you don't think that I'm just some crazy old crone. I also hope what I just told you would help you with your research of this town's history."

"Believe me, I've heard much crazier stories than this. That's sort of my job. And I believe most of them are true." I glanced at the photo in the frame again. "I'm sorry for what happened to your husband."

"Thank you." She sighed. "It took some time before I stopped having nightmares."

"Dolly, are those strange things still happening here?"

"Some. There have been strange animal attacks from time

to time, and a few people went missing over the years. But nothing as mysterious as before. I mean, not like what happened to Peter."

I got up. "Thank you so much for your time and for sharing your story with me."

"It was nice meeting you, Keira." She pulled herself up too and walked me to the door. "And," she added kindly, "I'm here if you have any questions."

Well, I knew this wouldn't be a vacation, I thought as I got in the car.

There were werewolves in this small charming town who left for a while. But now they were back, and I had to find their nest. If one of them killed Dolly's husband, I had to find him and put him down. That was our law. That was our punishment for premeditated murder. No matter how long ago it happened. From what Dolly told me about Peter's death, it didn't seem like an accident, and if that wolf had a taste of human blood, now that he was back he could strike again.

The fact that nothing much had happened here after Mom moved away told me that she secured this place from supernaturals before she left. She must've raised some protective barrier around the town. But if Dolly saw the werewolf again, then that could only mean the protection was broken, just like Mom's protective spell Dad was casting around me my whole life.

Was that a coincidence? No. It wasn't. The question was, how did it happen? That must've been a hell of a spell to keep supernaturals away from here for more than twenty-five years. To cast it, Mom had to evoke very powerful magic. Whoever broke it must've been just as powerful. So, who was it?

CHAPTER 8

The Lily House kitchen needed some cleaning, and on my way back, I stopped by the shop to buy dish soap and a sponge. My housekeeping skills were lamentable, but I preferred not to have dead flies in my food or crumbled plaster stuck to my fork.

"Take this one," said the same red-haired shop assistant who *interviewed* me when I stopped by yesterday. This time, she decided to follow me to the shelf as I stood eyeing the options with a six-pack of beer in my hand. She pointed at the one that said *Dawn Ultra Gentle*. "Something tells me you're not the type to use protective gloves. This one will do less damage to your hands."

"Martha?" called an elderly man standing next to the refrigerator. "Why is this fish on sale? What's wrong with it?"

"There's nothing wrong with it, Bernard," Martha rolled her eyes. She lowered her voice. "Not yet anyways." Then she added louder. "It's because there are only two days left before the date expires."

I grabbed the *Dawn Ultra Gentle* and a sponge and went to the cash register, followed by Martha.

She rang the items up, put the dish soap and the sponge

in a paper bag, and handed it over with a smirk. "Here you go, Miss X."

I pressed my lips together to suppress a smile. "My name is Keira. Keira Hale."

"See? Wasn't that hard, was it? So, Keira." She folded her arms under her breasts, rested them on the counter, and leaned forward. "Who's the Lily House ghost? Is it a man?" She whispered with a playful grin. "Is he young?"

The picture of plump Penny flitting around the house in her floral dress popped into my head. I chuckled. "Haven't seen it yet. I'll let you know if it shows up."

"PENNY, WHAT DO YOU KNOW ABOUT DARK ALLEY?" I ASKED, putting the paper bag next to the sink. "Dolly says it's shady."

"You met Dolly? She's still alive, then. That's good."

"Can't say the same about Ervin. He died fifteen years ago." I pulled one of the bottles out of the six-pack, then put the rest in the fridge.

"Really? You see, if I could visit the cemetery I would've known that. What about Laura?"

"She's in a funny farm."

"What?" Penny rose up from where she sat on the edge of the table. "Why?"

"No idea." I shook my head, uncorking the bottle.

I made my way outside, sat on the top stair shaded by the porch roof, and took a few gulps of beer.

"The bottle is still sweaty," Penny said, landing next to me. "Did you buy it from Martha?"

"Yep."

"*He* always bought it from her. The shop belonged to her father Henry when I was alive. But *he* said that Martha owns her father's shop now and has the coldest beer in town."

She still refused to say *his* name and I decided not to ask her again.

"So, what can you tell me about Dark Alley?" My gaze wandered around and stopped on the gate.

"Not much. Like Dolly said, it's one dark, creepy street. There are no houses there, just some old buildings. I went there only once. I was looking for my good-for-nothing husband. He used to drink. A lot. One night, when he came home, he started talking about some mysterious crap that even people from a place like Whispering Pines had a hard time believing. The next night, when he didn't show up until three a.m., I got worried. I was afraid he would go back there and get himself in trouble. So I went to check."

"What sort of crap?"

"I dunno." She shrugged. "He said that he saw a woman crouched behind a tree and sucking the life out of a dog. He said that she sensed him, and when she looked at him, she hissed and her eyes glowed red. He swore it was true and that the woman wasn't an ordinary human being.

"Back then I thought Ronny was losing his mind. But now . . . Look at me. I'm a ghost who's talking to you—a living, breathing person. And to be honest," she turned her head to look at me, "something tells me you're not an ordinary human either."

"Was *he*. . . I mean *is* . . . is *he* an ordinary human?" If Penny's *he* was my dad, I wondered if she knew he was a warlock.

"No. *He*'s a—" she frowned at me. "You're doing that thing again."

"What thing?" I made an innocent face.

"Trying to trick me, so I'll tell you who *he* is."

I laughed.

"Okay." I got up. "I need to clean that damn kitchen. Then, tonight, I will go to that Dark Alley and see what I find. Maybe your husband wasn't as gaga as you thought."

WHEN NIGHT FELL, I WENT TO THE BEDROOM TO CHANGE MY clothes. I couldn't go to a place like Dark Alley unarmed, and I needed to wear something practical to disguise my weapon. I put on my black jeans, a blue shirt, and my boots. Then I put the dagger in its sheath, stuffed it in one of my boots, and hid the handle under the hem of my pants.

There was a gun, a couple of stakes, and a small flashlight on the bottom of my now-empty suitcase sitting on the closet floor. I pulled it out and got the gun but then changed my mind. If what Penny's husband told her was true and there were supernaturals lurking on that street, then I had no clue what I was walking into. It could be one vampire or a whole pack of wolves. But I still had my magic, so I dropped the gun into the dresser drawer, took the flashlight, then pushed the suitcase back into the closet.

"Why would you go there? Seriously?" Penny grumbled, following me to the car. "People avoid that place for a reason."

"Penny, calm down."

As I got in the car, she stuck her head in through the open window. "Why risk it? If what Ronny told me was true, then that thing he saw is dangerous."

"Believe me," I started the engine, "if what your Ronny told you is true, then that thing is the one in danger."

"Oh really?" She threw after me with sarcasm as I took off leaving her head behind. "I thought you said you were a writer."

As I sped out of the gate, I threw a glance in the rearview mirror. Worried as always, she was hanging above the road with her hands nervously clasped over her stomach.

Dark Alley was at the edge of town. Since my plan was to search the area, I didn't drive there. I parked the car right before the turn to the alley in front of some old building attached to an auto repair shop called Billy's Garage.

After only a few steps down the alley, I felt it. A magical energy that made my skin hum. It wasn't strong, but it was there. I knew it was only an echo, and I kept walking, looking for its source.

The street was open for pedestrians, but I wasn't surprised they didn't come here for an evening stroll. And not only because it was dark with no lamp posts or lights in the buildings, but because the whole atmosphere and energy felt downright macabre. That was what scared the hell out of them, normal humans.

But I wasn't one of the normal ones. This was my job. And this time it was much more than work to me. This time it was personal, and I was hoping if I found what I came here for, it would get me one step closer to finding out who killed my parents and why.

I kept walking, pointing my flashlight at the bushes and into the dark corners of the buildings. Nothing unusual caught my eye, but the magical energy was getting stronger, and about fifty feet later, I saw a bright, yellow line of light radiating through the cracks around a door in the middle of a stone wall.

"There you are," I muttered under my breath.

It was a portal to another realm that couldn't be seen by ordinary humans. For me, however, it was just another door, and all I had to do was to open it and walk through.

The portal could be to the world of a one particular kind of creature or a gate to the supernatural side. After what Dolly and Penny told me, I was sure it was the latter. There could be anything behind that door. It could be a garden, it could be an empty room, a street, a store, or a cemetery.

Curious, I opened the door. I walked in and found myself standing in a room full of people. It was a pub. Busy drinking and chatting, not many of the customers turned to look at me. But the ones who did eyed me from head to toe.

Ignoring the prying looks, I headed to the counter. The vampire behind it narrowed his eyes. He wasn't wearing a shirt with the words *Free Bites* or showing off his fangs to help me identify his kind. I didn't need signs to tell them apart.

"You're new here."

"What gave me away?"

"You came in through the wrong door."

"Are you saying that the regulars don't use that door?" I sat on one of the vacant bar stools. "If so, then the door wouldn't be there, would it?"

"Right. Well then, who are you, beautiful?" He rested his arms on the counter and leaned forward.

"I'm a writer."

"And that must be your pen," said a male voice behind me.

I turned my head. The man was looking down at the handle of the dagger sticking out from my boot.

He glanced at the bartender and nodded to the side. The vampire moved to the other end of the bar. "What are you?" he asked. "I can sense a lot of power, but it's a bit hard to distinguish your kind."

"It's because I'm not a *what*. I'm a *who*."

"A *who* wouldn't be able to walk through that door. A *who* has no business here." He didn't sound rude but there was a little arrogance laced into his tone. "May I?" He pointed at the stool next to mine.

"Why ask?" I ran my eyes up his tall, strong body. "You made it clear this is your territory."

"Oh, you're welcome to stay," he said, sitting down. His gray eyes looked into mine, and I tried to ignore their beauty. "But you see," he continued, "this is a weapon-free zone."

"You don't say," I smirked. "So, what? You guys all leave

your claws and fangs home before coming here?" I glanced at the young woman on the other end of the counter. "And the band around that witch's neck must be a magic-blocking collar."

"I can assure you, this is a safe place."

"So you're saying, that a big bad wolf like yourself never gets his paws dirty?"

"Not here." The man frowned slightly. "If you don't believe me, try to use your powers."

I laughed. "Seriously? You think I'm that naive? No. I'm not gonna make it that easy for you. If you want to find out *what* or *who* I am, you'll have to work for it. I'll keep my cards close for a while, if you don't mind."

"When you say work for it . . ." With a smirk, he slowly moved his eyes down my body and then up to my lips. "Hell, yes. I'm all for it."

I chortled. "Not gonna happen. So far I don't see anything that could get you there."

He was very attractive, and he was perfectly aware of that.

He just looked down, laughing. "All right. Jokes aside. First of all," he held out his hand, "I'm Riven."

Inked into his forearm, the head of a growling wolf showed up from under the half-rolled sleeve of his shirt.

I took his hand and squeezed it. "That's good to know."

"Seriously? Do I have to work for your name too? Okay." He tapped his fingers against the wooden surface of the counter. "Then I'm sure you're here for a reason. What is it you want?"

"Well, first of all, I want to be served." That was the effect I had on most of them: they would suddenly forget simple things and mentally prepare for a *team deathmatch*. But it seemed Riven preferred to crack jokes to disguise his concerns.

"Right. Jackson," he called. "I'm sorry. With all this *poker game,*" he scoffed at the last two words, "I forgot my manners."

Jackson popped up on the other side of the counter. "What would you like to drink, beautiful?"

Riven gave him an annoyed look.

"What?" Jackson shrugged.

I tilted my head as I looked at the bartender. "Maybe he just disagrees with you?"

"That wasn't . . ." Riven raised his index finger. "No, that's not what I meant. I just don't like clichés."

"It's not a cliché if it's true," Jackson said with a grin, then addressed me again. "What's your poison?"

"And there goes another one." Riven rolled his eyes.

"A beer would be nice." I chuckled.

Jackson grabbed a pint glass, filled it from the tap, and put it in front of me.

"Thanks." I took a sip, put my glass down, and fixed my eyes on Riven's forearm. "Nice ink. Can I see it?"

Riven suddenly frowned like he remembered something. Then he heaved a breath. "Let me guess. You're the one who's staying in Esther's house, aren't you? You're Keira."

"And you wouldn't know that if you hadn't walked out that door."

"I can go wherever I want."

"You sure can. But should you? People don't come here, so maybe you should stay where you belong and leave them alone."

"We go for a run, for a hunt. Mostly at night. We don't touch humans. These woods are closer for some of us than the ones in our realm. You just go out the door and there it is, only a block away; the woods, the river. Some vampires get out there to feed on animals, but it doesn't happen too often since they have blood bag suppliers from different states."

"What about witches?"

"Some of the witches live in town, and we need them

from time to time. And sometimes, they need us. Our door is open for them, and vice versa. We also have human friends. But the ones who age slowly like my kind, or don't age at all like vampires, must disappear from time to time from the human world."

I sighed. "Usually after ten or twelve years. When people start asking what kind of products you use to keep your skin so fresh, or if you had some work done, or who does your botox."

"Are you speaking from your own experience?"

"Mmhm," I nodded slowly. "From my experience of kicking your butts back to your realms if you overstay your welcome."

"Aha. So you're a hunter," he stated with a smug smile.

"Congratulations," I sneered. "You passed the first level. But it only tells you what I do for a living and not *who* or *what* I am."

"Are you hunting someone in particular? For how much?"

"I'm looking for a killer. And this case is pro bono."

"Hmm." He pursed his lips. "Listen, yes, we go out there, but we're careful."

"Are you, though? Someone saw you, Riven. And that someone recognized you."

"I know." He sighed. "Dolly isn't young anymore, and it was dark. I hoped she wouldn't remember me."

"Seriously? After everything that happened, you thought she would forget?"

"Hey." Riven glared at me. "They're the ones who shot me. I would be dead if it weren't for Esther."

"She saved you?"

"Why wouldn't she?" He shrugged. "I didn't do anything wrong."

"You're joking, right?" I scowled at him. "You chased their kid all the way to the door, and then, only a week after

Peter shot you, he was found dead in the woods with bite marks and his flesh ripped open. Don't tell me it was just a coincidence. Or you're going to tell me it was the handiwork of raccoons?"

"So you think it was me? You think I killed Peter?"

"No?" I raised a brow.

"I'm not a saint. I've done things. But I've never killed anyone outside that door. Esther knew that. Otherwise, she would've sealed our way out ages ago."

So Mom trusted him. All of them. That's why she left their way to town open.

"Then why would you chase the boy?"

"Because that stupid kid stole from me."

"Stole from *you*? How did he manage that?"

"As I said, sometimes, our wolves go for a hunt in the woods. We detected something new lurking around. A couple of the wolves said that they saw some sort of shadows. They weren't as light as dark wraiths or gray and transparent like ghosts. They were ash black with a little shine, like burned wood, and they were denser. So I got curious, went looking for it, and when I shifted, I left my clothes and my watch under a tree next to the river. It was late, and I didn't expect people to show up in the dark woods at that hour with this town's reputation.

"When I returned from the run, I saw the kid and his friend going through my clothes. Keeping my distance, I growled to scare them off. Before they ran to their bikes, I saw the boy take my watch. I showed myself and growled again hoping he'd drop it, but he stared at me, then jumped on his bike and took off. So I chased him. I was trying to teach him a lesson and thought it'd keep him from going into the woods at night. But then Peter ran out and shot me."

After he mentioned the shadows, I barely heard the rest of the story.

"Let's get back to those shadows," I said. "Did you tell Esther about them?"

"Yeah. She said they weren't shadows but spirits. She said they're extremely dangerous, that they take over human bodies. A few days before Peter shot me, a young woman died from what the doctors said looked like a heart attack. But Esther said she didn't die from natural causes. She seemed sure the girl was possessed. She said those spirits are from a different dimension and the human body is not strong enough to survive their possession for too long."

Holy shit. Is that what happened to those two demons I caught in Atlanta? Does this mean they weren't really demons but they were men possessed by . . . demon spirits? So when I joked about the heart attack I was actually right.

"What else did Esther say?"

"Not much. She advised us to stay away from them, that we can't fight them and she's the only one who has the power to destroy them. She said she'd been hunting them for a while, and that she'd do her best to clear the town from them as soon as she could."

"And did she?"

"She must've. Because soon after that, she left, and we haven't seen those things anymore."

Was it possible those spirits followed Mom to New Orleans? Maybe that was the reason no one has seen them here since she left. Did Mom really get rid of them, or was it the other way around? What if they were the ones that killed Mom?

"Keira?" Riven's voice jerked me out of the stupor. My spacing out must've been all over my face because he asked, "Are you okay?"

"Yeah, I'm fine." I got up. "Thank you for telling me this. It was very helpful."

He bit his lower lip. "Does this mean I worked enough for you to tell me—"

"Not even close, but you're definitely on the right track. Keep it up and we'll see what happens."

I reached into my pocket for money to pay for the beer.

He raised his hand. "It's on the house. The least I can do for you not using your *pen* on me." Smirking, he glanced at my dagger again.

"Does this mean you own the place?"

"I do."

"Well, in that case, thank you for the beer." I winked at him and strode to the door.

CHAPTER 9

That night, I had trouble falling asleep. What I learned from Riven was more than I hoped for. If the demons in Atlanta were humans possessed by spirits, did it mean I had to go back and see if I could find them? And if I did, what then? How would I destroy them?

Mom told Riven she was the only one who had the power to destroy the spirits. Did I have that power? I had no idea, and no one out there could answer this question. At least, no one I knew.

I could see the dead now, and I wished I could talk to Mom. But, first of all, Mom didn't die here, and second, even if I went back to New Orleans, there was zero chance I would see her. She was too powerful of a supernatural being to still hover around, and Dad told me once that the supernatural's afterlife is completely different from a human's.

My dad sent me here to find answers. Had I learned enough to go back? Of course not. Something told me I'd only scratched the surface.

On my way downstairs the next morning, I smelled burned grease.

"Penny, what are you doing?" I asked, staring at the sink full of foam and the soap bubbles flying all around the counter.

She turned to me with a guilty smile. "I'm washing the . . . I wanted to make you breakfast but it didn't go well. I had a hard time grabbing the bacon with a fork and it sort of . . . well, burned. So I'm cleaning the mess I made."

"Are you sure you got enough soap?" I covered my mouth with my hand to suppress the laughter.

"Yeah." She pursed her lips. "I had a little accident with that too. But the coffee is good and ready," she added cheerfully. "Would you like some?"

She soared to the cabinet to get a cup, but I stopped her. "Thank you. I'll get it."

The *fun* didn't end there.

Later that day, I went to the great room thinking that if I was going to stay here longer, it was time to remove the sheets from the furniture.

The side of the sheet that was covering the tall, wide cabinet, got stuck at the top corner.

"Let me help." Penny flew up under the ceiling and looked behind the cabinet. "Oh, there's a little split in the wood." She grabbed the sheet by its side, but every time she pulled it up to unstuck it, she lost her grip on the fabric.

"Penny, stop. I can do it myself. I just need a chair."

I crossed to the nearest chair and the moment I pulled it to the cabinet, Penny succeeded. She bounced aside, lost her grip on the bloody thing, and the large dusty sheet fell on top of me, covering me to my toes.

"Aaaah," Penny fussed as I choked on the dust and started coughing. "Mmh, I'll go fill the bathtub with nice, warm water."

"No," I croaked, pulling the sheet off. "I don-have-ti . . ." I sneezed. "For a bath. I'll take a shower."

"Are you going somewhere?"

"Yes."

She pulled the sheet into her arms and dashed to the laundry room through the wall. As she vanished, the sheet fell to the floor.

"Dammit!" I heard her angry voice coming from the laundry room. "I keep forgetting."

You're forgetting because you're trying too hard.

Shaking my head, I headed to the bathroom.

After all those years of being a ghost, she knew the drill. Unfortunately, her excitement was working against her. She was so glad to have company that she tried to be as helpful as she could, to please me, hoping it would make me stay longer. Also, it seemed she missed taking care of someone. But since she hadn't needed to use all her skills before, she did need to improve some of them to get things done the way she intended.

After the shower, I drove to town. Before I left, I asked Penny to stop her cooking experiments before she burned down the house.

If I couldn't talk to Mom, I decided to contact another ghost. The young woman who died from a heart attack who Mom was sure was possessed by a demonic spirit. To do so, I needed to know her name and to make sure she was buried here in Whispering Pines.

I knocked on Dolly's door.

"Oh, Keira." She smiled.

"Hi, Dolly. I'm sorry for bothering you again so soon."

"You're always welcome. Would you like to come in?"

"Thanks, but I can't stay."

"Okay. Then, what can I do for you?"

"I need to ask you something."

She nodded. "Ask away, my dear."

"Around the time Peter died, there was a young woman who died from a heart attack. Do you remember her?"

"I remember." Dolly sighed. "It was Anabel's daughter. She was only twenty-one."

"Can you tell me her name?"

"Her name was Kate. Kate Carter. But if you wanted to talk to her parents, I'm afraid it's impossible. They're both dead too."

"No. I wasn't planning to. I just wanted to know her name and if she was buried here, in the town cemetery."

"She was. I take it you want to visit her grave." When I nodded, she gave me a warm look, and then added quietly with a sad smile, "You remind me of her so much."

"Me? I'm sorry, of . . . you mean . . ."

"Esther. You remind me of Esther."

I stared at her, my heartbeat rising. What did she mean? Was I that obvious? Or did Mom use to visit dead people because she could talk to ghosts too? Or maybe she found some resemblance.

My dad told me only once that I look like Mom. He said it wasn't my eyes or the other parts of my face. It was my look, my expression. And my hair was silver, just like hers.

"I see." Her smile still intact, Dolly nodded. "Don't worry, dear. Your secret is safe with me. Not everyone remembers her as I do. There aren't that many of us left in town who knew her as well as I did."

"Right." I cleared my throat.

Was it possible Riven noticed the resemblance too? That could've been the reason he was so friendly and open with me.

"Do you know how to get to the cemetery?" Dolly asked.

"No."

"It's on the other side of the river. When you pass Martha's store, take the right turn. There's a little bridge at the end of that lane."

"Yes. I know the bridge."

"When you cross it, just drive up the road and you'll see the first graves on the left side."

"Thank you."

As I headed back to the car, she stopped me. "Keira?"

I turned around. "Yes?"

She now looked serious, and even a little worried. "Are you here because it's starting again?"

"No." I shook my head. "I'm here to make sure it doesn't."

I PARKED THE CAR BEFORE THE IRON GATES AND STOPPED FOR A moment, listening to the silence.

The cemetery was bigger than I expected. Reading the names on the gravestones, I went deeper and deeper before I finally saw the name I was looking for.

What now? If there were ghosts here, shouldn't I be seeing them? But there weren't cloudy shapes flying around.

It was twilight, and I thought that maybe they were like vampires, sleeping during the day and coming out at night. But then I remembered that Penny never slept.

I've met witches and mediums who could communicate with spirits, but they never saw them. Having zero experience in contacting ghosts myself, I had no idea where to begin. So all I could think of was simply calling her name. Before doing so, I looked around to make sure there was no one else nearby.

"Kate?" I called. Nothing happened. "Kate Carter?" I said a little louder. My eyes traveled from gravestone to gravestone as I waited, hoping that the misty shade was hiding behind one of them and would finally decide to come out.

I've heard that most of the dead cross over, wherever that *over* was, and only some of them decide to stay behind, and they did it for different reasons. It was possible that a young woman like Kate was far gone. What gave me hope that she was still here was the way she died. If she was aware of what happened to her, then knowing how different and dangerous the other side could be might've scared her off from crossing over. Or, was it possible that, like Penny, she was somewhere—

Penny! I suddenly remembered that the first day I arrived, she said I made her turn on the light. Like if I had control over her. Then she said I shouldn't abuse my powers. Was it possible she wasn't the only ghost I could control?

I drew closer to the grave and said in a commanding voice. "Kate Carter, show yourself. Now."

She did. She slid out from under her gravestone, looking alarmed. "What do you want?"

She was a beautiful girl with big eyes and long silver hair which I supposed was blond once.

"Sorry. I didn't mean to scare you." I looked around again. "You're not the only ghost here, are you? Where are the others?"

"They are hiding from you."

"Why?"

"Because we can feel you. We can feel your energy. Some ghosts in this cemetery are centuries old. They know things. They said that you have power over the dead and you can make us do things for you."

"That's not why I'm here."

"No? I didn't want to come out but you made me."

"True. But I only did it because I need to ask you a few questions."

She frowned slightly. "About what?"

"About how you died. The doctors said it was a heart attack but I know something else happened."

"What if it was something else?" She shrugged. "You can't do anything about it, I'm already dead."

"So you do remember."

"Remember what? All I know is I was possessed by some nasty thing. And then I died."

"There must be more to it, Kate. If you tell me what you know, it could help me save someone else if it happens again."

"Does this mean they are back?"

"No. Not yet. But I'm afraid they're on their way, and I could use all the help I can get to protect this town when the time comes."

"Yeah." Kate's face turned sad. "She tried to protect it too."

"Who? Esther?"

"She said she'd help me. That she'd kill him and set me free. But I'm still dead."

"She spoke to you while you were possessed?"

"When she saw me, she knew at once that it wasn't really me. But she also knew I could hear her. She could've killed him right there, but she said if she did, I would die too, and that she needed time to find another way. The way that would help me survive."

"Could she see the dead too?"

"Yes."

"Did she come to you after you died?"

"Only once. To apologize for not being able to save me. But she never came back after that."

I sighed. "It's because she died too. Soon after you."

"She died?" Kate's eyes widened. "How? Did they kill her?"

"That's another thing I'm trying to figure out."

"If they got Esther . . ." she muttered, absently looking at the ground. "She was the only one . . ." She looked up again. "You can't fight those things."

"I'm going to try. But as I said, I need help to understand what they are."

"Nothing I say can help you. All I know is, it was inside me, but I wasn't gone. I was aware of everything he did and said while pretending to be me, but I couldn't do anything to stop him. Then I started disappearing. Fading away. And then it was like someone turned off the lights."

"How long did the possession last?"

"Only a few days. He said my body was young and he hoped it would last longer, but I wasn't strong enough. My heart gave away pretty fast. So in a way, the doctors were right. It was heart failure."

"I don't understand why it chose you. There must've been stronger women or men in this town who the spirit could use longer."

"That thing didn't care how long I'd live. If I died, it could jump into someone else. It chose me because it needed information about Esther, and it thought that a young and interesting girl like me asking questions would look less suspicious. People would find it easier and safer to share what they knew with me than with some dangerous-looking bulky wrestler. Luckily, people didn't know much about Esther, if she had a family or anything about some gate he was so interested in."

"A gate? What gate?"

"I have no idea." She shook her head. "Sorry, but that's all I know."

I ran my gaze around the cemetery again. "They don't need to hide from me." Then I looked at Kate. "Just so you know, you did tell me something I can work with. Thank you."

I smiled at her. Looking much friendlier, she smiled back.

When I arrived at the Lily House, as I came out of the car, I heard the sound of breaking China coming through the open kitchen window. I heaved a breath. Wondering what my Casper was up to this time, I headed to the door.

CHAPTER 10

What I learned from Kate Carter only added to the pile of questions I had no answers to. What was worse, I had no clue how to connect those multiplying dots—the pieces of golden talons, the spirits here all those years ago, the ones in Atlanta all those years after, and now some gate. Also, if it weren't the wolves, then who the hell killed Peter?

Dad said that the spell he cast around me was broken and I was in danger. If those spirits from another dimension were the ones that killed Mom and Dad, then that should mean it was me they were looking for when they came to Atlanta. But it seemed they had no idea who I was and were in Oliver Hancwell's nightclub to simply have fun.

The only explanation I could come up with was that the spirits knew the bodies they were possessing were about to die and were too weak for a fight. They didn't want to alarm me by showing themselves or revealing their purpose, or I might run and go into hiding. In that case, yay for me: their prudence didn't pay out and I disappeared anyway.

Now, the question was how long it would take for them to

find me again. Whatever time I had left, I hoped it would be enough to find the means to destroy them before it happened.

Thanks to Penny, I always had my coffee ready no matter what time I woke up. I filled a mug and put it on the island to sip my coffee while making myself a proper breakfast.

"Where are the pans?" I asked Penny, who was watching me hovering in the middle of the kitchen.

"There." She enthusiastically pointed at the bottom drawer of the island.

I pulled out two pans; one small, and another one a little bigger. The small one to make toast and the bigger one for scrambled eggs.

When I tried to make them for the first time, it took me a few attempts before they became edible. Now, they not only tasted good, but I could break the egg with one hand like Gordon freaking Ramsay.

"That looks great." Penny patted me on the back with her airy hand as I put everything on the plate.

"Thanks. I'm glad you approve."

"While you enjoy your breakfast, I'll go check on the plants. There are a few in the backyard that are still alive and could use a little watering."

"Take your time," I muttered, but she was already past hearing me.

Using my Penny-free time, I once again went through the information I'd gathered so far. But I still had nothing I could grab onto. Then I thought, now that Dolly knew who I was and I didn't have to pretend with her anymore, I could ask her more questions about other accidents that happened around here, or if she'd heard about this mysterious gate Kate mentioned.

The more I knew, the closer it would get me to the

answers to the most important questions; why the spirits were after my mother and how to destroy them. If they were the ones responsible for my parents' deaths, then clearly Mom's work on finding the way to kill them without killing the host wasn't finished, otherwise, I was sure she would've killed them when they attacked her.

I dropped my empty plate into the sink and went to the study. Witches usually had grimoires, and I wondered if Mom had one.

I made my way to the glass-door cabinets under the wall and opened one filled with books. On the middle shelf in front of me, there were a couple of old books on gardening. Mom was interested in gardening? I remembered the dried-out flowerbeds I saw on my way to the backyard.

The next book that caught my attention was an emerald-colored hardcover in the same color box. The writing on the spine said *The Waterlilies* by Henry S. Conrad. The moment I reached for it, Penny popped up next to me.

She looked worried.

I dropped my hand. "What is it now?"

"Keira, there's something wrong with the pond?"

"The pond?" My eyebrows shot up. "What do you mean?"

"I think it's drying out."

"Penny," I squinted at her. "What the hell are you talking about? It's summer, and it's hot, but it's not that hot."

"Come on, I'll show you." She darted away through the wall, then popped next to me again. "I'll come with you."

I rolled my eyes. "I know the way, Penny."

As we reached the pond I stared at the water. "It looks fine to me." I shrugged. "Care to explain?"

"I noticed the change a couple of weeks ago, and I've been watching it since." She pointed her finger at the edge of the pond. "Look. There was always grass around it, but then the dry edge started showing up. At first, it was only a few inches. Now, it's almost a foot deep."

I ran my eyes around the perimeter. She was right, there was definitely a dry rim around the pond. "So you're saying this has never happened before."

"Never. At least, not in my nearly twenty-five years here."

"I could Google it," I said hesitantly. I didn't think that I would find anything that could help me to slow down the evaporation.

I headed back into the house. By the time I got there, Penny was already waiting for me in the great room where I'd left my laptop the previous night.

"There you go," I said, pointing at the screen showing her the search result. "*Evaporation*," I started reading aloud, "*causing water levels to drop roughly one inch per week. Evaporation is the most common cause of pond water loss. But don't panic, this is normal. Factors such as location, time of year, pond size, and especially weather, can affect the rate at which evaporation occurs.*"

"Evaporation?" Penny said doubtfully. "We've had hotter summers than this one. Why did it never happen before?"

"You're a ghost. How do you know if it's hot or not?"

"I may be a ghost, but I'm not stupid," she said resentfully. "There's a thermometer outside the kitchen window."

I felt bad as I looked at her pouted lips. "I'm sorry, Penny. I didn't mean to . . . Let's give it a little more time, okay? I think Google is right and there's no reason to panic. At least, not yet."

"Okay." She nodded. "I'm just worried about the lilies. I don't want them to die."

"Aaand you're panicking again. There's still a whole pond of water, Penny. Nothing is going to happen to the lilies."

An hour later, I was sitting on Dolly's couch, who once again welcomed me into her home with a warm smile and a glass of iced tea and cookies.

"So how are you doing in that house?" She sank onto the couch across from me. "People say it's haunted. Is that true?"

"Not really. It must be the creaking stairs that scared kids away."

I wasn't sure why I lied. But then I thought it was the right thing to do. If I told Dolly I had a ghost, she would definitely ask who it was, and I would have to lie anyway since I wasn't sure if Penny would want me to tell the others she was the one haunting the Lily House.

"I hoped you'd stop by," Dolly said. "I was wondering how it went in the cemetery. Was Kate there?"

"Yes, she was there."

"Oh, poor girl. I was hoping she had crossed over."

"Dolly, do you know what she really died from?"

"I do. After what happened to Peter, Esther confided in me. I was only a few years older than her, and we became friends, but unfortunately, not for long. She told me that Kate didn't just die from a heart attack. She said Kate was possessed by a dark spirit and her body wasn't strong enough to contain it. Did Kate confirm this?"

"She did. And I believe that's the reason she's still here. I didn't ask her, but I think after what happened to her, she was afraid she wouldn't end up in what we call a *better place.*"

"But she didn't do anything wrong." Dolly looked at me, sad and confused. "Why wouldn't she? What happened to her wasn't her fault."

"Of course not. But that kind of darkness leaves a spot on the human soul. I'm not an expert, but she must've felt something that scared her away."

"Do you think it's possible to fix this? To help her cross

over?" Dolly looked at me hopefully. "I mean, do you have such power?"

"To be honest, I don't fully understand my powers yet. I've always been a witch, but I never saw ghosts before I came here."

"Keira." She bit her lower lip, then asked timidly, "Did you see any other ghosts at the cemetery?"

I heaved a breath. "You want to know if Peter is still here. Sorry, but I don't know. Kate said that there are more ghosts at the cemetery, but they were afraid to show themselves to me."

"Why would they be afraid of you? I thought they would be happy to have someone who could help them communicate with the living."

"Because it seems I can control them. Kate didn't show up either until I ordered her to. They're afraid I would use them to do my bidding."

"But that's silly. What on earth could ghosts do except haunt houses or scare people sometimes at the cemeteries?"

I thought of Penny, who'd been pinned to the Lily House for a quarter of a century paying back a favor to *him* and who I was sure did more damage to that house in the last few days than all those years she'd been haunting it.

"You'd be surprised," I chuckled. "But don't worry, I wouldn't do that to them. All I need from a ghost is information that could help me to keep this town safe," I hurried to reassure her. "Dolly, since you know who I am and why I'm here, I thought maybe it would be okay if I asked you a few more questions."

"You can ask me anything, Keira. I'll help you as much as I can."

"Did you ever hear Esther—"

"My dear," Dolly smiled. "I think you can call her Mom now."

"Right," I gave a curt nod. "Kate told me the spirits were

interested in some gate. Did my mom ever mention something like that?"

Dolly locked her hands in her lap and leaned forward. Her eyes narrowed, looking into nowhere as she rummaged through her memory.

Then she finally said, "No, sorry, I don't think she did. Sounds important, though."

"It does, doesn't it?" I sighed.

"And you have no idea what it could be?"

"No." I shook my head. "Dolly, do you know anyone else my mom helped with problems like yours? I heard about Ervin, but he's dead. And there's Laura, who's in a mental health center."

"Who did you hear that from? Was it Martha?"

"You mean the store owner?"

"So you've met her."

"Yeah, I've been to the store a couple of times. But no, I never talked to her about any of this. Do you think I should?"

"I thought she might've asked you a few questions herself. She's one of us who was aware of Esther's abilities and remembers her as well as I do. I'm sure she's already figured out who you are."

"She's pretty chatty. And yeah, I got the feeling she might know more about me than I was planning to reveal."

"Don't worry. Martha likes to talk, but she wouldn't tell people more than what you told her yourself. And speaking of Laura, I think it's what happened to her all those years ago that messed up her mind. If I'm not mistaken, she was possessed by a spirit like Kate."

"What?" I stared at her. "How is she still alive, then?"

"That I don't know. But your mother has been working on the problem, and who knows, maybe in the end, she came up with a solution. And if she did, then it must've been right before she left, because I'm sure she would've shared the good news with me."

Or maybe she wasn't sure yet that it was good news. What if she was testing whatever she came up with to see if it was working or not? If Laura was already possessed, then she would die anyway, and Mom probably tried to save her the only way she thought possible.

"Is that mental health center somewhere around?" I asked.

Dolly smirked. "I'll write down the address for you."

CHAPTER 11

The mental health center was fifteen miles away from the town, and I drove there right away.

Dolly said that Laura had no family, at least not in Whispering Pines, and all she knew about Laura's condition was that she didn't talk to anyone except herself, muttering some incoherent words under her breath from time to time.

I didn't know what I was hoping to find from someone who wasn't in her right mind and hadn't talked to people for seventeen years, but she was the only one who I knew had survived the possession, and I had to give it a try.

I parked the car in front of the old stone building with a green roof, got out, and headed to the glass double doors. The spacious foyer was almost empty. I passed by a visitor talking to a nurse on the couch and approached the reception.

"Hi. I'm here to see Laura Baker."

A young woman looked up at me from behind the computer. "Let me check, please." She looked at the computer screen again, typed a few words, then smiled. "That will make Laura's day. She hadn't had visitors for years."

"Yeah, I've heard. Could you please point me to the visiting area?"

"No need. She's in her room. But first, could you write down your name here?" She opened a journal and put it in front of me.

A nurse led me to Laura's room. She opened the door, and my eyes stopped on the back of a wheelchair. Above it was a head with shoulder-length gray hair. I moved forward, glancing around. A bed and a nightstand with a big lamp sat on one side of the room, and a small sofa with a painting hanging on the wall took up the space of the other side.

"Laura, dear," said the nurse, approaching her, "you have a visitor. There's a nice young lady here to see you."

Smiling, the nurse gave me a nod. As she left, I rounded the wheelchair.

Laura absently stared at the window in front of her. The light cotton dress she wore did little to hide the shape of her withered body.

"Hi, Laura," I said, leaning against the window sill. "I'm Keira."

She turned her foggy green eyes at me, and her indifferent expression changed at once.

She frowned, then her eyes widened and she muttered, "It's you."

I'd never interacted with mental patients before, but I'd seen in movies that they often confused their visitors with someone else. Apparently, someone they wanted to see.

"You're probably mistaking me for some—"

"Esther," she hissed, frowning again.

I gaped at her. "I'm not—" But before I could say another word, she interrupted me again.

"You said you'd fix this. You said—"

"I'm not Esther." I straightened up. "I'm her daughter. Esther died twenty-five years ago."

She looked down and went silent for a moment. Then she muttered under her breath, "Then there's no hope."

"Hope for what?" I asked, my heartbeat rising.

When she looked up at me again, her eyes weren't green anymore. They were pitch black and she spoke in a different, raspy voice. "Oh, it's not over yet. She can do it. She can get me out of here."

What the bloody hell? Was that thing still inside her?

"Laura," I dropped to one knee before her. "Laura, can you hear me?"

Her eyes turned green again and she nodded slowly. "I can't take this anymore. She said it would give me control over him and I just had to wait a little until she found a way to get rid of him for good."

"You mean the spirit. It's still inside you," I said, more to myself to make it sink in. "But how? No human could survive the possession for that long."

"She said she found a way. I was okay for a while. But then . . . I started losing time. Like I could be in a store one moment, and the next, I was home and I had no idea how or when I got back. It didn't happen often, but the doctors were afraid I would one day forget my way home and get lost. They thought I was in danger and that I could end up hurting myself. When I tried to explain to them what was going on, they locked me up here." She heaved a deep breath. "This thing has been messing with my mind all this time. What Esther did helped keep him from completely taking control. But a couple of weeks ago, something changed. It's like he was asleep and then suddenly woke up. And now, he manages to take over more often."

"Oh, God. Laura, I'm so sorry. If only I could . . . I'll try to—Wait. You said *what Esther did.* Laura, what did Esther do? And do you remember how she did it?"

She nodded again. Then she reached for the small buttons

on her dress. She unbuttoned a few of them and showed me her chest. There, above her heart, was a Satan's star burned into her skin. It looked exactly like my father's mark.

I got up from my knees. I was speechless, and I needed a moment.

"Laura, listen to me." She looked up at me. "You can't give up. Do you hear me? I need you to fight this thing a little longer. I can't promise you to get rid of it tomorrow." I wasn't even sure if I would be able to do it in a month, or ever. "But what I can promise you is that I'll do everything in my power to find a solution to this problem."

Her face softened. "You're just like her. She always tried to help people."

"Then I'm sure you know that she would've helped you, she would've kept her promise if she was still alive."

"Yeah, I believe she would've." She sighed.

"Also, you need to get out of this room, talk to people, and participate in whatever they do to entertain you all."

"I can't. Like I said, I ended up here because I started talking about it, and when I got here, I made that mistake again. I tried to explain to some of these people what was going on with me. No one believed, of course. So I tried to keep away. I've been talking to this thing, cursing it, fighting with it all this time, and they think I'm crazy. I've been locked up here long enough with my thoughts to believe it myself. And now, after all these years, I'm afraid of not only talking to someone but even leaving this room."

"Start slowly. You can do it. A little bit every day. Laura, you need a distraction. And stop talking to him. He feeds on your anger and despair. The more you ignore him, the weaker he'll get."

"It seems easy when you say it, but it's not." She shook her head.

"I know it's not. That's why it's called a fight." I sighed.

"You have to fight for your freedom. And the first step is getting out of this room."

"Okay. I'll try," she whispered, and I saw a little spark in her foggy eyes. "Thank you. For coming. Your visit alone gives me strength."

THIS WAS TOO MUCH AND I WAS OVERWHELMED. DRIVING HOME, I couldn't stop thinking about the mark. To make sure I wasn't mistaken, I grabbed my phone and found the picture I took of the one on Dad's chest. The image proved that I was right; the marks were identical.

Now the question was, when did Dad get it and how? If Mom was the one who burned the mark on Dad's chest, then that would've meant he'd been possessed for twenty-five years. But I didn't believe he was. Maybe he wouldn't have drowned in the darkness like Laura since he was stronger and he was a warlock, but there would've been signs in his behavior and darkness in his mind. Besides, there was no way Simon wouldn't have seen the mark during all those years.

Was it possible that the mark was meant not only to control the spirits but also to prevent possession? In that case, if Dad found out about the spirits, he could've burned it onto his chest himself.

But if he knew about the spirits, wouldn't he mention it in his letter to warn me? I remembered him saying in the letter, *Apparently, I was on the right track and it didn't end well.* Maybe he found out about them at the last moment.

My head buzzed. *All questions and not a single answer.*

Back in my bedroom, I pulled Dad's letter out of my bag and read it one more time. I already knew that there was nothing there about the mark and I didn't find any hint on the spirits either.

But after everything I'd learned since arriving in Whispering Pines, the letter did sound different to me. And one particular part made my blood run cold.

I don't know until this day what happened. All I know is that she was attacked in an alley, and by the time I got there, Simon's parents and Esther lay dead on the ground. Esther died from injuries, but Simon's parents had no wounds. I didn't get a chance to examine their bodies and I assumed they were killed by powerful magic. I supposed whoever was hunting Esther had finally found her.

"Simon's parents had no wounds," I repeated under my breath. Did this mean they were . . . If that was so, then they must've been the ones . . .

I yanked the phone out of my pocket and found Richard's name in my contacts. My boss had connections to official law enforcement agencies, and he could help me to get the proof to the first part of my theory.

"Richard, hi. It's—"

"Keira? Hi. Didn't expect to hear from you so soon. Are you coming—?"

"Richard, I need your help."

"Help? What sort of help?"

"You know my mother was killed."

"I do. And I'm sorry the same happened to your father, Keira," he said with compassion.

"Listen, I'm trying to figure out who is behind it, and I need my mother's autopsy report and the two others who died with her—Elisabeth and Jason Walker."

"They were killed in New Orleans, if I'm not mistaken."

"Yes, and I would try to get it myself, but I'm not there right now."

"I understand. I know you don't like to ask for favors, and it means you're asking me because you have no choice. But, Keira, it happened a long time ago." Richard sighed. "I don't know if—"

"Yes, I know that. That's why I need you to pull some strings for me. Richard, please. I don't need the report itself, I need to know what it says about the cause of death. They weren't killed by humans, and it's sort of our job to find out what happened, isn't it?"

"You don't need to convince me, Keira. I only meant the people I knew then might not be there anymore. But I'll see what I can do."

"Thank you, Richard." I hung up.

Of course, I could ask Simon to go to the police station and try to get the report himself. But then, he would read it, come up with questions himself, and insist on coming to help me. I didn't want to reopen his wounds or learn the truth, and his coming here would only put him in danger. I wouldn't let anything happen to him. This wasn't his fight.

"Keira?" Penny's voice came from behind the door.

"What is it?"

"Someone just walked through the gate. A man. You want me to scare him away?"

I looked out of the window. It was dark, but I recognized the silhouette. Riven. "I'm afraid you'll die trying."

"I'm already dead."

"You know what I mean. And relax. I know who he is."

The question was, what the hell was he doing here in this hour? I put the letter in the dresser drawer and headed downstairs.

"Sorry for showing up like this," Riven said as I opened the front door. "I would've called first, but we forgot to exchange numbers."

"Oh, he's handsome." Penny clapped her hands, beaming. "Are you two—" She stopped talking the second I gave her a look.

"I'll let you two chat." She darted away through the open door, more of fear than politeness.

I looked back at Riven, who was eyeing the lily carved on

the wooden bar above the door and didn't seem to notice my distraction.

"Just tell me it's not bad news. I got tons of that already and no clue what to do with it."

"I'm afraid it is. And you better sit down."

Crap.

"Come in." I artistically waved my hand toward the foyer.

He walked inside, stopped, and ran his eyes around. "Wow. After all these years, it looks almost the same."

"So you've been here before."

"Yeah. Mostly for the same reasons I'm here now. You know? To solve supernatural problems."

I headed to the kitchen, and he followed me.

"What sort of problem brings you here this time?" I pointed at the chair, inviting him to sit at the table, then sat across from him. "How bad is it?"

"Oh, it's bad. One of my wolves went for a run last night. And when he came back, he said he saw it again."

"It?"

"The spirit."

"Fu—!" I shut my mouth. I got up, went to the fridge and pulled out two beers. "It didn't take long, did it?" I muttered under my breath, putting one of the bottles in front of Riven.

"Well, it has been at least twenty-five years since—"

"For you. Yes. But I'm pretty sure I met a couple of them only a week ago. In Atlanta." I removed the cap from the bottle and took a few large gulps.

"And you didn't destroy them? Oh, wait, I forgot." He raised a brow and fixed his gray eyes on mine. "You're just a writer."

"Cut the crap, Riven. You know who I am."

Nodding, he bit his lower lip to suppress a smile. "I knew Esther got married, but I never knew she had a daughter. The shade of your hair was enough to make the connection. It's not just silver. It has this special glow. Then, after we talked, I found even more resemblance."

"The hair, yes. But I never thought I looked like her until Dolly said she knew who I was just by looking at me."

"Are you as powerful as she was?"

"I've no idea, okay?" I snapped. "I was always afraid to fully use my powers. And I don't know how powerful Mom was or what she knew because, you see, she was killed before I was old enough to be able to ask, or even speak properly."

"I'm sorry, Keira." Riven sighed. "But she must've left some records, a grimoire, something? You could ask your father. Or is he an ordinary human?" Riven gulped some beer.

"My father." I gave him a short, mirthless laugh. "I arrived here right after his funeral."

Riven squeezed the bottle in his hand. "God, Keira. I'm so sorry. I shouldn't—"

"Forget it. And the answer to your question is no, he wasn't just a human. He was a powerful warlock. He was killed, like Mom. But it seems everything that happened here, Mom kept to herself. He didn't know much, and all he left for me was a letter, telling me to come here. Said it would help me find some answers. So far, all I've found is more questions. I'm buried under them."

"You're a hunter, Keira," said Riven quietly. "You'll figure this out. And you're not alone. My pack and I—we'll help you as much as we can."

"*Your* pack?" I smirked. "Don't tell me you are an alpha."

"Why?" Riven chuckled. "Don't look old and respectable enough?"

"Oh, I think you're old enough," I teased him. "And stop asking me about the look. I'm not one of your wolves to flatter you, so you'll get no compliments from me."

He laughed.

There was a moment of silence as we sipped our beers, and then he asked, "So what do we do about this spirit?"

"That's the problem, I don't know. I've no idea how to destroy them. You said it yourself: Mom was the only one who could kill those damn things. Did you see her do it? Did she use a weapon, some unique sword, or was it some spell?"

"No. I've never seen her destroy a spirit. But Keira, you're her daughter, and you probably have the same powers. How about we try to find this thing first?"

"Then what? What are we going to do? Glare at it to death?"

"Then you can practice on it, use your powers, and see which hex affects it the most. You have to try. Maybe fail once or twice, but then try again and eventually find the way."

Why not? I could do that if they don't kill me first. Or worse—possess me.

"If they're already here, then I don't have time for experiments. But I don't think I have a choice. You're right." I sighed. "I have to try."

"They? You can't be sure this is one of the two you saw in Atlanta. It could be a stray."

"Girl can hope," I scoffed. "Otherwise, it means there are more of them out there and they could possess half of this town in no time."

"Then we should get going."

"Can you track them?"

"No. I don't know their scent. But Paul, the guy who saw it, can. We'll take him with us. Come on." Riven got up. "It's hunting hour."

I looked down at my short skirt. "If we're going into the woods, I need to change."

He gave me a curt nod. "I'll wait outside."

The moment I walked into the bedroom, Penny popped up next to me.

"Penny, house rule number one?" I never came up with

rule number two, so her not entering my bedroom was the only rule so far.

"Oh, sorry. But . . ." She flew out the window, then turned around and poked her head into the room. "Are you leaving?"

"Yes." I pulled off my skirt.

"For how long?"

"I don't know." I picked up the jeans hanging on the back of the chair with my jacket. "And, Penny, you're still in my room."

"I know, but . . . I'm just worried. You haven't eaten anything. You should eat before—"

"You worry too much." I put on the jeans and my leather jacket. Then I rummaged in my purse and fished out two protein bars. I always had them on me in case I had a long day at work. "Here." I showed the bars to Penny, then stuffed them into my jacket pocket.

"That's a snack." As I rolled my eyes, she added quickly, "But it's better than nothing."

She followed me outside.

"Who were you talking to?" asked Riven, who stood leaning on the hood of my car.

"No one." I gave him a suspicious look.

"You do know wolves have great hearing, don't you?"

"I do. But you couldn't hear me unless you were listening. So maybe you shouldn't be eavesdropping?"

"It's true, then." He grinned. "The house *is* haunted. And you can see and talk to ghosts?"

"Nope. I was talking to myself."

"Don't worry, your secret is safe with me. Who's the ghost?"

"Can't tell without permission." I cleared my throat. "But I have to warn you; it's very protective."

"That's right," Penny thrust her fists into her sides.

Suppressing a chuckle, I passed by Riven and got into the car.

Riven slid onto the passenger seat. "Don't tell me it's a man. Is it? You live with a man ghost?"

"Are you jealous?"

"Is he a human ghost? Or some—He didn't die in the shower in his birthday suit, did he?"

"God, you're worse than Martha." Chuckling, I shook my head. "Your guess is even more ridiculous than hers."

CHAPTER 12

Riven, Paul, and I spent half of the night searching the woods, but every time Paul caught the scent, he lost it again. And it happened close to town the last time, which wasn't a good sign.

"What happens if the spirit possessed someone? Would you still be able to catch his scent?" I asked Paul.

"I doubt it. The humans' scent is strong, and if it blends with the spirit's, it will become a different scent, and I would only notice the change on someone I know well."

"We'll come back tomorrow and try again," said Riven as we headed back to the car. It was parked on the shoulder of the road not far from the cemetery. That was the point closest to the woods where Paul saw the spirit.

Five minutes later, I stopped the car in front of the door to Riven's pub on Dark Alley.

"Thanks for the ride," said Paul, getting out.

"Would you like a drink?" Riven asked.

"No, thanks. Maybe another time."

He turned in his seat to face me. "Are you sure?" He looked into my eyes and raised a brow. "I thought you might need a pick-me-up."

"What I need is a put-me-down. I'm no wolf, you know. Spending half of the night in the woods after a long day makes me tired."

"Put-you-down sounds good too." His shoulders shook from silent laughter. "I would be happy to do that for you if you let me."

"Funny," I chuckled back. "Remember the ghost? It's not only protective, it worries a lot. I gotta go or it'll think I'm dead."

I wasn't exaggerating. I drove into the front yard through Penny, who was hanging in the middle of the road right in front of the gate.

"I was so worried," she started the moment I got out of the car. "That guy, he's not an ordinary human, is he?"

"No. He's a werewolf." I thought it's time to enlighten her.

"I knew it! Are you okay?" she spluttered, following me inside. "He didn't bite you or anything, did he?"

I heaved a sigh. "No. He is a good werewolf." I opened the bedroom door, walked in, and gave her a look before closing it. "And you're going to be a good ghost, be quiet, and let me sleep."

Something was buzzing. With my eyes still closed, I moaned. "Penny, that's it, you're going to hell. I'll send you there myself."

The buzzing continued. I pried open my eyelids, glanced at the nightstand, and realized it wasn't Penny. It was my phone.

I focused my blurry vision on the screen and saw Richard's name. I scooped up the phone and pressed the green button. "Hey."

"Hey, Keira."

"Any news?" I asked, sitting up.

"Yeah. Fortunately, the New Orleans agency still has a couple of people I had a few drinks with once or twice. The detective I asked for a favor didn't send me the report, but he pulled the info and filled me in."

"What did he say?" I asked, my heartbeat rising.

"Your mother . . ." Richard cleared his throat. "She had stab wounds. Three. But here's the thing; they didn't find the weapon, and they're not sure what she was stabbed with."

"That sounds mysterious." I knew she was stabbed, but I didn't know anything about a missing weapon.

"And it gets even more mysterious with the other two who I thought were killed with her. It so happens, they didn't have any wounds at all, so they weren't killed. They just died from heart attacks."

"Dammit," I muttered as he said what I was so afraid to hear.

"And there were no witnesses. So since the police didn't have much to work with, they got stuck, and after six months, the case was closed. Keira?"

"Hm?"

"Doesn't it remind you of something? Something that happened with those two demons you caught before you left?"

"Yeah, I'm afraid there's a connection."

"What sort of connection?"

"Those two men weren't demons. They were humans possessed by spirits. The human body can't survive the possession for too long, and at some point, their heart stops."

"What?" gasped Richard. "So that's what happened? Then where did the spirits go? Doesn't it mean they could be possessing someone else?"

"Don't worry, Richard, I'm working on it."

"Keira, those two people that were found with your mother . . ." he sighed. "Do you think it means . . ."

"Yeah." My heart sank. "I'm afraid so. I just wish I knew what kind of weapon they used to kill my mother. Obviously, it wasn't just a kitchen knife, or the forensics would've figured it out."

"No, it wasn't. The skin around the wounds had dark marks, and so did the wounds. He said the knife burned through. It looked the same if someone was stabbed with a hot poker."

"Maybe it means that the weapon was witch-made." I heaved a breath. "Thanks for your help, Richard. And just in case, tell James to keep his eyes open."

"I will. Take care, Keira."

One question from my long list was answered. I found out what happened to my mother.

And that was the answer I feared the most.

Simon's parents were possessed by the spirits, and they were the ones who killed my mom. That's how the spirits tricked her. They possessed the two people Mom was closest to. If she killed the spirits, she would've also killed her friends. She would never do that, and that's how the spirits overpowered her when they attacked her in that alley. That's what got her killed.

The spirits were after my mom, and she's the reason Simon's parents died. If Simon finds out, it'll break his heart.

Did Mom have the stamp she used to burn the mark on Laura's chest with her in New Orleans? She probably did. If she'd used it on Simon's parents, it would've given them more time with their son. But the spirits must've cornered her, and I was sure she didn't carry that thing around with her.

With Dad, it was different. He was killed in our house and the stamp must have been somewhere around.

If he knew about the stamp, why didn't he mention it in his letter?

Apparently, I was on the right track and it didn't end well. I remembered his words. It probably meant he only found out about the spirits and what the stamp was for *after* the spell he cast around me was broken.

It had probably been in the safe with the other things he'd left for me, but it seemed that after he marked himself, he never got the chance to put it back.

So what happened to it? Did the spirits take it? They could've. If Dad used the stamp right before he died, the spirits wouldn't leave the key to their prison cell just lying around.

THERE WAS SO MUCH I STILL DIDN'T KNOW, BUT THERE WERE TWO very important questions I had to find the answers to as soon as possible. Mom said to Riven that the spirits were from a different dimension. The first question was, where was that portal they came through, and the second—how could I destroy them?

There had to be something in this house to help me find the answers, or at least a hint to point me in the right direction.

I spent the whole afternoon going through Mom's books, checking out the cabinet drawers in the study, then in the great room hoping to find a grimoire or journal.

"What are you looking for?" asked Penny.

"Do you know some other place in this house where Mom could've kept her personal things?"

"Well, theres some stuff in the third-floor room."

"The third floor?"

"The attic room," Penny added.

I remembered when looking from the outside, the house did have an attic that looked like an extra story.

"Show the way."

Penny soared up to the second floor, and as I caught up

with her, she led me to a door next to the bathroom which I had thought was a broom cupboard. I opened the door and saw a staircase. On the top of it was another door.

I climbed up, opened the door, and walked inside. It was one big room with a low ceiling illuminated by light coming in through two small, dirty windows. Pieces of old furniture were set up as a sitting room, and here and there were a few boxes.

"I didn't do much cleaning here," said Penny. "So I'm afraid it's a little dusty."

"It's not that bad since the windows were closed." Though there were lots of cobwebs under the ceiling and around the lamps.

I opened one of the boxes. It was filled with winter clothes.

"Are those your mom's things?" Penny asked.

"Yeah, it looks like it."

"Well, then maybe it's better I leave you alone. To have another moment."

As she left, I looked through the clothes and pulled out of the box a sweater. It was long and thick, and still in good condition.

I checked out the rest of the clothing, then put the sweater back and opened the box beneath it. This one contained some old tableware.

The box next to it was stuffed with books. I picked up the one on the top, then another one, but none of them looked like a grimoire. The third book had something between the pages which I assumed was a card Mom used as a bookmark. But when I pulled it out, my eyes froze on the image.

It wasn't a card. It was a photograph of Mom. She was sitting on the bench in the backyard of this house. Behind her was the pond. She was smiling. The back of her hand was resting on her folded legs, and in her open palm sat a white lily.

A sigh skipped from my lungs. She did love this place.

I made a note to myself to check on the pond from time to time, though I doubted there was anything I could do if it was really drying out.

I went through the rest of the boxes but found nothing even remotely close to what I was looking for, and all I carried out of that room was Mom's photograph. I returned to my bedroom and put it on the dresser.

CHAPTER 13

I heard the roar of an engine and turned to the window. A motorcycle stopped at the gate. Judging by the driver's gentle shape and the long hair falling down the shoulders from under the helm, it was a girl. She reached for the postbox and put something inside. Then she gave the house an appraising look and took off.

"You got mail." Penny popped up in the window.

"That's strange," I muttered. Who would be writing to me? No one knew where I was.

"I'll get it for you." Penny dashed to the gate and returned a few seconds later, holding a small envelope. "There's no name or address on it," she said, handing it over.

I glanced at the back of the envelope. It was blank too. I found a note inside.

Her eyes fixed on the envelope, Penny lingered behind the window. To satisfy her curiosity, I read the note aloud.

"Keira, I'm making roast chicken tonight and if you're not busy, I invite you to join me for dinner. Dolly."

. . .

"THAT'S NICE OF HER," SAID PENNY. "YOU'RE NOT BUSY, ARE you?"

"Tonight, Riven and I are going to the woods again."

"You're going into the woods with that attractive werewolf? This doesn't sound suspicious at all." She chuckled. "The house isn't good enough for him?"

"Don't be silly. We're looking for something."

"Like what?"

"Like dark spirits that can possess people."

"Oh, God. I heard of those back when I was alive but I refused to believe. So it's true, then."

"Yeah. I need to find them and see if I can destroy them."

"But of course," she said with notes of sarcasm in her voice. "Because that's what writers do. I can't believe you'll drop all this writing you've been doing to search for some spirits."

I gazed at her.

"What? You're going to punish me for speaking the truth?" She gave me a startled look. "What happened to the freedom of speech?"

"I'm not going to . . ." I turned my eyes to the ceiling.

"I thought by now, you know . . ." She shrugged, then added in a smaller voice, "You could trust me enough to be honest with me."

"Okay." I spread my hands. "I'm obviously not a writer. And as you guessed before, I'm not an ordinary human. I've got some powers, and I hope they'll help me to fight those spirits."

"What sort of powers?" Penny's face lit up with excitement.

"Magical powers." She opened her mouth, but I raised my finger before she could say another word. "No. No more questions."

"Okay," she sighed. "No questions. So what about Dolly?"

"That's another one." I turned around and headed to the hallway.

"Yeah." Afraid to break the rule, she didn't follow me, but flew away from the window and then back into the house through the wall of another bedroom down the hall. "But it's not like I asked you if you could throw fireballs. It's a normal, human question. I think you should go. It will make Dolly happy." She kept talking as she followed me downstairs. "You've had enough frozen pizzas and could use a nice homemade meal."

"I would love some roast chicken." I sighed. "I think I could squeeze that dinner into my schedule. I have a couple of hours." Riven was trying not to be seen by people, so we had decided to go to the woods after dark, when most people were home.

Dolly was nice to me, and I didn't want to turn down her invitation. And I suspected that she was curious about my visit to Laura.

I DIDN'T WANT TO GO TO DINNER EMPTY-HANDED, SO ON MY WAY to Dolly, I stopped by the store to get something for dessert.

Luckily, Martha was busy with a customer, and it gave me time to browse the shelves without her hovering over me like another Penny.

I glanced over the pastries, then at the range of chocolate bars and boxes, and as I proceeded to the fridge with cupcakes and cakes, the voice behind me said, "Expecting guests tonight?"

I decided it was the right time to finally use nosy Martha for advice. "Do you know what Dolly would like with her tea?"

Martha chuckled. "Are you bribing her for information or something?"

"For information?" I glanced at her then turned my eyes back to the fridge. "Does this mean I have to bribe you to get an answer?" As she chuckled again, I went on. "She invited me to dinner. I want to bring her something she actually likes to save her a trip to the trash."

"Let me see." Martha pulled open the fridge door. "Depends on your wallet. She drools over this chocolate cake but can't afford it more than once every few months with her pension. But if you want something less—"

"Great. Pack it up."

"I like you." Martha pointed her finger at me. "You should come to my store more often." She pulled out the cake and headed to the counter.

I paid, took my cake, and started toward the door, hoping to get out before she came up with some snarky comment.

"So how's the writing going?"

I could tell she was smirking.

"Not good. I'm procrastinating."

"Damn. It looks like you need a little push."

"YOU DIDN'T HAVE TO," SAID DOLLY, TAKING THE CAKE OUT OF my hands. "I'm glad you could make it."

I followed her to the kitchen, inhaling the delicious smell of homemade dishes. "Thank you for inviting me."

"I would've called, but I didn't have your number, so I asked the neighbor's daughter to deliver the note."

"That was nice of her."

"Yeah. She didn't mind. She loves riding her motorcycle."

"Can I help you with something?" I asked, looking around.

But the kitchen was clean, and there was no trace of

cooking.

Dolly put the cake on the counter. "Everything is ready." She pointed at the two dishes on the table covered with foil. "Here." She handed me a bottle of wine. "You do drink wine, don't you?"

I nodded. "I do with good food. And as people say, a meal without wine is called breakfast."

Dolly chuckled. "I hope you like red. The opener should be in that top drawer." She pointed at the drawers under the counter.

I looked into the top one. It contained the cutlery. Then I pulled open the one below and found the opener among the spatulas and large spoons.

I watched Dolly set the table as I uncorked the bottle. Always relaxed and calm, today she seemed fidgety to me.

"Where did I put the glasses?" She looked around. "Oh, there they are." She grabbed them where they sat ready on the counter. "I knew I had them somewhere close."

"Dolly, are you all right?"

"Oh, yes." She put the glasses on the table for me to fill up. "I'm just a little excited. You know?" She shrugged. "Lately, I rarely have company for dinner."

"Yeah. That makes two of us."

The difference was, I was okay with that and Dolly wasn't. She missed having people around and probably felt lonely and abandoned. I wondered how often her son Tony visited but didn't dare to ask. It could be a touchy subject, and she was already a little fussy.

She removed the foil from the dishes, and we sat down.

"That looks great," I said, watching her cut through the crunchy golden coating of the chicken.

"Help yourself." She reached for her wine, and I followed suit. "I don't think I've said this yet, so here it goes. Welcome to Whispering Pines, Keira. I'm glad you showed up."

"Thank you." I smiled as we chinked glasses.

"How is it?" she asked, watching me take a sip.

"It's pretty enjoyable."

"I don't understand much about wines."

"Neither do I. As long as it's not too sour it's good for me." I put some chicken on my plate and then added a spoonful of roasted vegetables.

"So how did it go last night?" Dolly took a sip from her glass, then put it down and grabbed a piece of chicken with her fork.

"You mean my visit to Laura?" I asked, even though I was sure she knew nothing about my searching the woods with Riven.

She fixed me with an absent look, then she shook her head the way people do when trying to catch up with a conversation after they spaced out. "Yes. Why? Did something else happen?"

"No," I lied. It wasn't like Dolly could come and search the woods for the spirits with Riven and me, or help with the current situation in any other way, so there was no need to sow panic. "Laura is in much better condition than I expected. It appears she's not as crazy as people think." I sent a piece of chicken into my mouth.

"How do you mean?"

"When she was first admitted to that place, she tried to explain what happened to her. Obviously, no one believed a word she said, and they all assumed she was crazy. Since then, she hasn't seen the point in talking to people, and she prefers to stay away from them. She opened up to me only after I told her who I was."

"Did she tell you anything new?"

I considered my answer and decided to keep it simple. "No, all the same things I learned from Kate."

I expected Dolly's next question to be about the most important detail: how did Laura survive for so long? But the question never came.

Something was bothering me, and it started the moment I walked into the house. I got distracted by the food and wine, but now that strange feeling was coming back, and I threw around a searching look.

"Is there something wrong?" Frowning, Dolly followed my gaze.

"No. I just thought I heard something," I lied again.

"Must be the neighbors." She waved her hand toward the yard.

"Right. I don't have those, and I think I'm getting used to the peace and quiet."

"I'm sure you had neighbors where you came from. New Orleans, was it?"

"Atlanta. I haven't lived in New Orleans for a long time. But yes, I had a building full of them. And pretty noisy ones."

I told her a funny story about one of my encounters with my neighbor, and we started sharing our good and bad experiences.

But as soon as Dolly served the dessert, she steered the conversation back to our supernatural problems.

"Keira, did you discover anything new about the gate?"

"The gate?" I swallowed the piece of cake in my mouth. "No. I don't think it will be easy, since no one I've met so far has heard of it, and I haven't found anything in my research in the house either."

"That's strange. Esther must've left some clues for you to—"

My phone buzzed. "Sorry, but I need to take this."

It was Riven.

"I'm at your house. Are we going or not? Where are you?"

"I'm with Dolly and . . . I lost track of time. I'll be right there." I hung up. "I'm sorry, Dolly, but I have to go."

"Did something happen?"

"No. I just promised to meet someone." I was trying to be as honest with Dolly as possible, but I couldn't tell her yet that I was meeting the same werewolf that chased her son once, was shot by her husband, and who she thought was responsible for Peter's death. First I had to tell her all about the werewolf and clean Riven's name from this unfair accusation. And now wasn't the time.

"Thanks again for having me," I said as she walked me to the door.

"It was my pleasure. Let me know if you find anything out about that gate."

The moment I stepped out on the porch, I felt lighter, like some weight was lifted from my chest. Though I couldn't explain why. Spending time with Dolly had never been a burden for me, but she seemed a little off today. That could be the reason for this discomfort.

"I will." I glanced back at her. "See you soon, Dolly."

CHAPTER 14

I was in Atlanta, in a hospital, walking down the corridor with a nurse. She looked startled, and so did the patients. They rushed into their rooms and shut the doors the moment they laid their eyes on me.

The nurse led me to the elevator. We walked in, and after a short ride, she led me to the morgue.

"Which one?" I asked.

The nurse pointed at one of the refrigerator drawers and hurried away. I opened the drawer and pulled out the stretcher with the corpse covered with a white sheet. I didn't know how, but I knew it was a woman, and I wanted to see her face. I reached for the edge of the sheet, but before I could pull it off, a rough voice thundered above me. "It was your fault. It was all your fault."

I bounced back, and the next second, I was in the bathroom of my Atlanta apartment, standing in front of the mirror.

"No," I gasped, staring at my pitch-black, bottomless eye sockets.

I sat bolt upright in my bed.

"Oh, thank God," Penny breathed out with relief. "It took me a moment to wake you."

"Why? What happened?" I looked down at the beads of sweat on my chest.

"You were having a nightmare. You were muttering things I couldn't understand. What was it? What did you see?"

I remembered the corpse and the words, *It was your fault. It was all your fault.*

No. No, it wasn't. It was just a nightmare. I didn't do anything.

I looked up at Penny. "It was nothing. I'm fine."

She looked at the empty glass on my nightstand. "Would you like some water? I could get it for you."

"No, thanks. And Penny, what are you doing here," I shifted my gaze around, "in this room?"

"I heard . . . I got—"

"Let me guess. Worried?"

She sighed. "Coffee is ready," she murmured and drifted away.

I pushed the pillow up and leaned against it.

"It was just a nightmare," I repeated under my breath.

After two more nights of searching the woods with no results, I was becoming restless, that was all.

But on second thought, it could be a warning. Maybe something was about to happen, and if I didn't stop it, people would get hurt.

It would be my fault.

THAT NIGHT, INSTEAD OF SEARCHING THE WOODS AGAIN, I DECIDED to visit the cemetery and ask Kate if she'd seen anything.

"Yes, it was here two nights ago." Kate nodded. "But I haven't seen it since."

"Are you sure it was only one?"

"Yes."

Then maybe Riven was right, maybe it was a different spirit, not one of the two from Atlanta. On one hand, that was a good thing. It meant they didn't follow me here and I still had time to figure out how to destroy them before they found and killed me like they killed Mom. But on the other, it was bad because it meant there were more of them.

"Kate, is Peter Benson here? Dolly's husband?"

She didn't reply but glanced back. I moved forward, reading the names on the gravestones, and she followed. But before I could find the grave I was looking for, a male voice spoke behind me.

"How is she?"

I turned around. The ghost of a man around forty glided toward me.

"She's fine," I replied. "I had dinner with her a couple of days ago."

"She hasn't visited for a while. I was afraid she was sick or something."

"Peter, I know you miss her," said Kate. "But you've been here long enough to know that with time, people visit the dead less and less. It doesn't mean there's something wrong with them. On the contrary, it could be a good thing."

"She misses you too. I can feel it in her voice every time she talks about you," I said to comfort him. "Wait. If you don't see her until she visits, does this mean you can't leave the cemetery?"

"That's right," said Peter.

"To leave the cemetery, we need the freedom of the dead," said Kate. "The older ghosts said Esther was the one who could give us that freedom, but she did it before and realized it was a mistake."

"Why?"

"Some of the ghosts had grudges to settle and they started

haunting people and houses. People were scared, started having horrible nightmares and visions, and many of them came to her for help to get rid of the problem. She gathered all the ghosts back to the cemetery with one command, and the ones who'd done real damage vanished. That's another reason the other ghosts are scared to show up to you. They're sure Esther didn't send those ghosts to the better place, and they're afraid you could do that to them too."

"Me?" I poked myself in the chest. "I didn't even know she could do that." I stared at Kate and then at Peter. "But I'm sure she did good things as well. I mean for the dead."

"She could help us cross over. Can you do that?" Kate asked with longing in her voice.

"I have no idea. If she could do that for you, why are you still here?"

"I never asked her."

"And neither did I," said Peter. "I thought I'd wait for Dolly so we could cross over together. But I don't know what will happen now that Esther is gone."

"I'm sure there's a way. I'll look into it." This all was very new to me. But if Mom could help people cross to the other side, maybe I'd be able to also after I learned more about the afterlife. "Peter, there's something I need to ask you."

"You want to know who killed me." He predicted my question. "I have to tell you it had nothing to do with those spirits."

"No. But all this time, Dolly thought it was the man you shot."

"You mean Riven, the werewolf?" He shook his head. "It wasn't him. It was a werefox. A big one, I should say."

I stared at him. "A werefox? Are you sure? I haven't seen one for a long time. They're rare and hard to come by."

"Yeah, that's what Esther said too. She said the fox wasn't local and that she'll deal with her. And I believe she did, because I haven't seen that werefox since."

I wondered if Riven knew about this.

My head jerked back toward the town at the sound of a cry. Or more like a wail. "What was that?"

"A banshee," said Kate.

"A what now?"

"Yeah," she sighed. "Someone is about to die."

"Does she wail every time people die?"

"No. Not every time. She only shows up when it's someone supernatural or if the death is caused by one. They're not dead yet, but it doesn't take long after her first wail."

"I gotta go." I rushed to my car.

What could've happened? What if it was Riven, or Paul, or another werewolf who decided to come out for a hunt, ran into people, and got shot? It could also be some other kind who came out from the portal in Dark Alley to take a stroll.

Or maybe it was the other way around? What if one of them hurt someone in town? It was my job to prevent these sort of accidents and protect people from the rule-breaking, dangerous creatures.

Banshees wail close to the place where someone is about to die. Following the cry, I drove toward the bridge.

What was going on? I'd seen many things, but I'd never seen ghosts before, not until I arrived at Whispering Pines. And now a banshee? I knew banshees existed, but I'd never seen or heard one. Where did these new abilities come from? And why now?

I crossed the bridge, drove by Martha's store, then took a turn, and the cry got closer as I continued down the familiar street.

No. It can't be.

The skeletal body of a woman with long silver hair, wearing a long, flowing silver dress, hovered a few feet above the road in front of Dolly's house.

I stopped the car, got out, and ran up the porch stairs.

Terrified, with my heart beating in my throat, I knocked on the door.

"Dolly?" I called. Just in case, I tried the handle, but the door was locked. "Dolly, are you there?"

I heard footsteps, and the door opened.

"Keira?" Dolly stared at me. "Is everything okay?"

"I was going to ask you the same thing. Dolly, are you okay? You're not sick or injured, are you?"

"No. I'm fine." She took a step back. "Do you want to come inside?"

"No. I just . . ." By the look on her face, I could tell my behavior alarmed her and I had to come up with an explanation. "I was at the cemetery, and . . . I saw Peter."

"You did?" Dolly's eyebrows moved up, but she didn't react the way I thought she would. A few days ago when she asked me if I'd seen her husband, she teared up. Now she looked pretty calm. "So he's still here?"

The banshee's cry pierced my ears, and I decided to cut this conversation short.

"Yes, he is. He says hi. He said you hadn't visited him for a while and he was worried if you were sick. So." I shrugged. "I thought I'd come check on you."

"Thank you. If you see him again, tell him I'm fine and I promise to visit him soon."

"Yeah, I'll do that. I'm glad you're okay. Good night, Dolly." I stretched my mouth into a smile and headed to my car. I heard Dolly close the door, and I glared at the banshee. "What the hell are you doing here?"

She stopped wailing and fixed me with her creepy red eyes. The creep factor increased when she spoke, showing off her black teeth. "You're new here, but you must know I'm a harbinger of impending doom. I'm—"

"I know what you are." I cut her off. "I'm asking why you're here, on this street?"

She drew closer. "This is a warning. To you." She pierced

me with her gaze. "I'm doing my job and you need to do yours, or you'll see much more of me."

"A warning? What do you . . ." But she was gone before I could finish my question.

Another puzzle. I felt a spasm of fear in the pit of my stomach.

I returned to my car, got in, and sat there, watching Dolly's house.

I was a hunter, and I was good at my job in Atlanta. And not just there. Every time the agencies in other big cities needed help, they asked Richard to send Keira Hale. I knew all the portals to the other realms, and I could hunt down any supernatural, registered or not.

However, here I felt lost. This little town was full of mysteries. Too many things were happening at the same time, and they were all new to me. I had no doubt that eventually, I'd get to the bottom of this. I just needed more time. But the appearance of a banshee made it clear that time was a luxury I couldn't afford.

The lights in Dolly's house went off. I started the car and headed to Dark Alley. I needed a drink. A real one.

This time, everyone in the pub stared at me as I made my way to the bar.

"Hi, Jackson." I sat on the stool.

"I'm flattered." The vampire grinned, baring his fangs.

"Huh? By what?" I squinted.

"You remembered my name."

"Well, it's not just your name." I decided to *flatter* him more. "You're hard to forget." I released an artificial sigh.

Jackson burst out laughing. "What would you like to drink, beautiful? It's on the house."

"Whiskey, please. Large."

"Large whiskey coming up!" he exclaimed enthusiastically. He filled the tumbler, put it in front of me, and leaned over. "Rough day?"

"I've had worse." I took a big gulp of my whiskey, then drew my face closer to Jackson's and whispered, "Jackson, why is everyone staring at me?"

"You see, now they all know who you are."

"Do they? Did Riven—"

"No." Jackson shook his head. "He didn't have to."

"Is it a good or bad stare? I can't tell."

"It's both. We had great respect for your mother, Keira. But we also feared her a little. And the fact that you're a hunter—"

"Okay." I pointed a finger at Jackson and shook it. "Riven was the only one who knew that."

"No. Not the only one. We have connections to other realms, and we do visit each other from time to time. After we learned your name . . ." He tilted his head. "You're pretty famous out there."

Suddenly, the world seemed pretty small. I gulped the rest of my whiskey. "Don't worry, Jackson, I'm not gonna kill you." I raised a brow. "Not until you kill someone first." With a thud, I put down my empty tumbler.

Jackson reached for the bottle and filled it up. "I'm clean, my lady." He put the bottle aside and leaned on the counter again. "We might rip each other's throats in here, but out there, in the human world, we are as cute and fluffy as bunnies."

"She knows that." Riven showed up next to me and sank onto the vacant stool.

"I know she does." Jackson reached for another tumbler. He filled it with the same amber liquid and put it in front of Riven. "She's just had a bad day."

"Hey, Jackson," called a vampire from the end of the counter. "I need another one." He raised his empty pint glass.

Riven turned on his seat and rested his elbow on the counter. "Keira, did something happen?" he asked quietly.

"Not yet," I replied, watching Jackson fill the pint glass

from the tap. "But I'm afraid it's about to." I reached for my tumbler.

"What makes you think so?"

"Too many signs." I skipped the details. The tale about the banshee and my creepy dream wasn't a good bedtime story. "It's just . . ." With my eyes on my drink, I shook my head. "I arrived here to figure out who killed my parents. But it looks like this little town planned a much bigger job for me."

"You're not alone. As I've told you before, I'll do everything I can to help you."

"Thanks. But first, I need to figure out what exactly the job is."

What I was sure of, whatever that job was, being a hunter wouldn't cut it. It would require a witch. It would make me tap into the magic I refused to use for so many years.

I LAY AWAKE FOR A LONG TIME. BANSHEES ARE HARBINGERS OF death. She said she was here to do her job, and she was right in front of Dolly's house. Kate said they only show up for supernatural deaths. Was Dolly in danger? And if she was, could I still save her?

I couldn't stop thinking about my dream. If only I could see the dead woman's face in that morgue. The voice telling me it was all my fault echoed in my head over and over, and every time I closed my eyes, I saw those pitch-black eye sockets staring back at me from my reflection in the mirror.

CHAPTER 15

I picked up my phone from the nightstand to check the time. 10:23 a.m. I had a headache, but I knew it wouldn't last long. However, the stench of alcohol wouldn't just go away. I pulled myself up and headed to the bathroom to take a shower.

I heard Penny humming something downstairs.

"You already showered." She eyed my wet hair as I climbed down the stairs fifteen minutes later. She was folding laundry on the great room's couch. "I'll change your bedsheets today."

"You're not my house elf, Penny. I can do it myself."

She followed me as I walked by her to the kitchen.

"What's a house elf?"

Once again, I had to remind myself that Harry Potter was after her time.

"It's from a . . . It's those little elves . . . You know what? You should read more books. You're so behind on everything." I grabbed a mug from the shelf.

"I read all the novels I could find here. Twelve books altogether. No romances. It looks like your mom wasn't much of a romance reader. But I loved *The Hobbit* and *Alice in Wonderland*."

I filled the mug with coffee and headed outside.

"Keira?" Penny appeared before me as I stepped out onto the porch. "I would love to read something. Something with a romance in it. Could you get me something? I mean, from the library?"

"The library?" I glanced at her askance. "I'm not going to the library. There are people there, and I'll have to make a card. No way. I already have one Martha to annoy me with her questions, I don't need more Marthas."

"Please." The corners of her mouth slid down.

I heaved a breath. "I'll see what I can do." She was bored, and she could use some entertainment. "The fridge is empty, so I'll have to go to town anyway."

"Thank you."

It was hot. I sat on the step in the shade of the porch roof. Penny drew closer and landed next to me.

I thought of the ghosts at the cemetery. They were pinned to that place just like Penny was pinned to this house, but at least they got to see their loved ones from time to time when they visited them.

"Penny?"

"Hm?"

"Did you have kids?"

"Yeah. A daughter," she replied in a small voice.

"Where is she now? Does she live here in town?"

"No." She shook her head. "She left as soon as she finished high school. She couldn't stand Ronny. His drinking was driving her crazy."

"Where did she go?"

"Boston. She found a job in a coffee shop, and that's where she met her husband." Ghosts couldn't breathe, but Penny's chest heaved as if she inhaled deeply.

"Did she keep in touch? When did you see her last?"

"When she came to visit my grave."

"I'm sorry, Penny. I know you wish you were still at the cemetery so you could see her again."

"Would I?" she said sadly, her eyes fixed on the dry flowerbed. "I was there for about four years before *he* moved me here. She visited me twice the first year I died. And that was it. When she came the first time, she spoke to me. She said she was getting married. The second time she stood there, pregnant, said she came to sell the house. And that was it. She never came back after that. It made me sad, of course. But I tried to understand. Husband, kids, new life. You know?"

My heart squeezed from guilt. I stopped by Mom's grave after Dad's funeral before heading to Simon's bar, but in all the years I lived in Atlanta, I hadn't visited it once.

"I'm so sorry, Penny," I said.

"I'm fine." She gave me a weak smile. "I love it here. It's so much better than a bunch of ghosts and tombstones. This is my home. At the cemetery, the sad ghosts talk about their old lives over and over. Here I get to talk to the living who have something new going on every day."

I smiled. "And how often does that happen? Aren't *he* and I the only ones who can see you and talk to you?"

"Yes. But when *he* visits, he leaves me a lot to think about until his next appearance. You haven't been here long, but look how much has happened already. I know that not all of those things are good, and you have a lot on your mind right now. But with you here . . ." She gave me a warm look. "It's like I'm alive."

"Then you should know—you're my first roommate."

We both laughed.

MARTHA LOOKED THROUGH SOME PAPERS WITH HER GLASSES hanging off the tip of her nose.

"It's been a few days. Are you out of frozen pizzas?" she asked without looking at me as I walked into the store.

"That too. And I need a frame for a photo. Do you have those here?"

"Honey, this is a grocery store." She gazed at me over the top of her glasses. "There's a Home Decore at the end of this street, right before you reach the town square." She dropped her eyes back to her papers.

"Thanks." I headed out.

"You forgot your pizza," she called after me.

"I'll be back."

The Home Decore was a small store, but it had a little of everything to adorn the house interior: candles, paintings, vases, artificial plants, and souvenirs. There was more, of course, but those were the things that caught my eye when I glanced in through the window.

The bell tinkled above my head as I pushed open the door. There was no one inside except the shop assistant.

At the sound of the bell, the young woman looked up from her phone. "Hi." She smiled.

It wasn't the ordinary welcoming smile that hits the faces of service workers on autopilot every time they see a customer. This was a broad, genuine smile. Though I couldn't tell what exactly it meant. Was it an *Oh, look who's here,* or was it an *Oh, thank God, I got a customer*?

"Hi." I smiled back.

"What can I help you with?" The woman came out from behind the counter.

"Do you have picture frames?"

"Sure." She beamed wider. "Here, let me show you." She led me to a shelf with frames of all sizes. "What size do you need?"

"Let me see." For my mom's photograph, I had only two

options: the gray frame and the brown one. I chose the brown one. It looked warmer.

"Anything else?" the woman asked.

"No. That's all."

She wrapped the frame in thin white paper and put it in a small paper bag.

"Is there a bookstore nearby?" I asked.

She beamed again, handed over the bag, and pointed out the window. "It's right across the street."

"Thanks."

Like my mom, I wasn't a romance reader either. That's why, after one glance at the books, I called the shop assistant to help me out. The young man ran his eyes up and down the shelves, then asked me how steamy I preferred my novels.

"Oh, no." I quickly shook my head. "I mean, I don't know. They're not for me. They're a . . . a present for a friend of mine." I shrugged. "She's around fifty and very romantic."

Five minutes later, I came out of the bookstore holding a bag with three romance novels.

On my way back to Martha's store to get my groceries, I drove by Dolly's house to make sure she was okay. She was outside talking to a neighbor, but I didn't stop to say hi, thinking that my checking on her every day could make her suspicious and nervous.

"You got books for me?" Penny shrieked like a teenager. She grabbed all three of them at once when I put them down on the kitchen table. But they were big and probably a little heavy for her, and the bottom one slammed back on the table. "These are brand new." She raised her eyebrows. "You bought them? Oh, Keira, you didn't have to."

"It's no problem. I asked for help picking them out, so I hope you like them." I had a lot of thinking to do, and I hoped the books would keep her busy and quiet.

I was right about the *busy* part. She said she'd go read a little and disappeared into one of the bedrooms. I didn't see her for hours. But the *quiet* part was a little too much to hope for. Wherever in the house I was, I could hear her, "Oh noooo," or, "That's right, you piece of crap," or "Oh God," or her loud giggling.

After a little snack, I took the frame out of the bag and went upstairs. I looked through the half-open door of Penny's room on the way to my bedroom.

She lay on her side on the bed, or pretending she was, her hand supporting her head over the open book before her. Even though it was still light outside, she had turned on the lamp, and it looked like she even tried to throw a blanket over her legs to create a cozy atmosphere that fell flat through her incorporeal body. The whole picture, and the fact that she was too invested in the story to notice me, brought a smile to my face.

I walked into my bedroom and picked up Mom's photograph from the dresser. I placed it in the frame and held it in my hand for a moment, looking at my mom and the lily sitting in her open palm. She tried so hard to keep this town safe, and I didn't want to let her down. I glanced at the pond behind her, then put the frame down and headed to the backyard.

My heart sank as I looked at the dry rim around the pond, now about two feet deep. Even stranger, the connection to it I felt before was now much stronger.

The water was evaporating too fast, and I couldn't come up with a reason for it. I wondered if anybody else in town had a pond. My first thought was to ask Dolly, but then I thought maybe this time I could ask Martha.

I knew if I did, there was a chance Martha would bombard me with questions followed by her usual sarcastic comments. But the thing was, with her, it was much easier, since I already trained her not to expect answers.

With Dolly, however, it was different. She was friendlier. She was open with me right from the beginning, and I tried to be the same. And that was the problem. I couldn't ignore her questions. And I didn't want to disappoint her with my answers, or the lack of them. Like that question about the gate.

And that was another reason I didn't want to go to her right now.

During dinner, she kept asking me about the mysterious gate the spirits were so interested in, and I had no idea what to tell her, since I was sort of busy with other problems and hadn't given much thought to that one yet. If I went to her now and she asked about the gate again, I had nothing —*Why was she interested in . . . Oh my God . . . Was it possible that. . . ?*

The sudden, terrifying thought hit me like lightning. I dropped down on the bench and grabbed the edge of my seat. I tried to remember Dolly's behavior and our entire conversation during dinner a few days ago.

First, the cake. Martha said Dolly loved it, but when Dolly opened the box and saw it, she didn't react at all. It did seem strange to me back then, and I thought Martha must've pulled a prank. If Dolly loved that cake, wouldn't she say something like, *Oh, that's my favorite,* or *How did you know?*

Then she seemed nervous for no reason at all. And she didn't called me *dear* that day like she always did before. Not even once.

When she asked me to open the wine, she said the opener was in the top drawer, but it wasn't there. A woman her age would know exactly where she kept things in her kitchen, especially one who lived alone for so many years and had no one to mess up her drawers.

Another thing that didn't seem right was when I told her about my visit to Laura. When Dolly first told me about her, we both wondered how she survived the possession for so long. I expected her to ask more questions on that subject, but she never did. Instead, she kept asking about the gate.

And last night, she was just as passive about the fact that I saw her beloved husband's ghost.

And how the hell did she know about New Orleans? I never told her anything about where I came from or where Mom moved when she left Whispering Pines.

As I went through every detail piece by piece and put the puzzle together, the whole picture changed. That day was the first time I felt strange in Dolly's company, and there was a reason I felt relieved when I finally walked out onto the porch.

Because it wasn't Dolly in that house. Not anymore.

I ran to my car.

CHAPTER 16

It was getting dark, and I turned on the headlights as I drove through the woods.

The second the lights illuminated the road, I hit the brakes and gripped the wheel to brace myself. The banshee hovered in the middle of the road and gazed at me through the windshield with her red eyes.

She released a high-pitched, lamenting cry.

I clenched my teeth, stepped on the gas, and drove right at her. But before I could reach her, she vanished.

"No. You can't take her. I won't let you," I kept muttering under my breath as the car sped down the road.

After what seemed like forever, I finally stopped the car in front of Dolly's house and threw myself out. But as I darted for the front door, I stopped.

What if I was too late?

I reached for the door knob, turned it, and pushed the door open in what felt like slow motion.

"Dolly?" I called quietly.

In response, I heard a loud wail.

I didn't look back at the banshee but walked into the house.

I didn't have to go far. Dolly lay on the floor in the middle of the living room, eyes open.

"Hello, Keira," said a voice that didn't sound at all like Dolly's. "I knew you were coming."

"Get out of her," I hissed, glaring at the pitch-black eyes that gazed at me.

"Or you will do what?" the spirit scoffed. "I chose her because I knew you would never hurt her."

"Dolly?" I knelt next to her. I shook her, hoping she was still alive. "Dolly, can you hear me?"

The spirit flew out of her. "No, she can't," it sneered. "She's been dead for almost an hour. I only stayed because I wanted to see your face when you discovered how helpless you are against us."

Piercing the black eyes with a glare, I got to my feet. I put my palms together, rubbed them against each other, and separated my hands. Electrical currents sparked between them.

The spirit dashed to the door. I spun around and threw my hands before me, sending electrical waves at him. Captured by the currents in the doorway, the spirit went into convulsions. He was fighting, trying to get free, and I forced more magic into my palms to keep my grip on him. Though the spirit's form was denser than a ghost's, it was still difficult to grab onto and harder to retain, and it was slipping away. After a few more attempts, it broke free and was gone.

I lowered my shaking hands. The banshee, who had been silent for a moment, moved closer and wailed again.

"Shut up!" I shouted. She obeyed, though I didn't understand why. "Leave. Now." She gave me a barely perceptible nod and was gone. Or was it a bow?

It took me a moment to look back into the room and face my defeat. My eyes scanned the room, but Dolly's ghost was nowhere to be seen. That meant the spirit was telling the truth; she was dead long before I got here. I drew closer to the body lying on the floor, knelt next to it, and closed her eyes.

"I'm sorry," I whispered, looking at her pale face. "I'm so sorry."

I pulled my phone out of my pocket and called 911. Then I sat on the floor under the wall to wait for their arrival.

The image of the spirit kept flashing in front of my eyes. Its appearance surprised me. It looked nothing like a ghost. It was about six feet tall, ash colored, and glowed like burned wood. And it was denser, just like Riven had described. I'd never seen anything like it in my life.

"Is Dolly okay?"

I turned at a female voice coming from the threshold. It was a girl, the one who I supposed delivered Dolly's invitation for the dinner to my house. Except now I knew that it wasn't Dolly who sent it to me.

"No." I shook my head.

The girl came forward and gasped as she saw the body. "Oh, my God. Is she dead?"

I heard the siren of the ambulance.

More neighbors gathered around the porch, trying to catch a glimpse of the body. I, however, remained inside to answer the medics' questions.

I told them I came to visit and found Dolly dead on the floor. Then I watched them examine the body, put it in the black bag, then the stretcher, and then into the ambulance.

As the blinking lights of the car disappeared behind the corner, I went back inside to find the keys and lock the door. I looked on the hallway table, then I checked its drawer.

The keys were there, lying on a piece of paper that looked like a receipt. I picked it up. It was a bill from a restaurant for a roasted chicken and vegetables.

I remembered the clean kitchen when I arrived for dinner and the dishes ready on the table. Apparently, spirits couldn't cook.

Wishing I could talk to Dolly one last time, I locked the door, got in the car, and headed to the cemetery.

Dolly wasn't buried yet, so unless she'd already crossed over, her ghost was supposed to be in the house. But since I didn't know much about the afterlife and my theory was based only on things I'd heard and read, I needed to talk to someone with firsthand experience.

Kate showed up the moment I walked through the cemetery gates. "She isn't here," she said.

"No?" My heart sank. "I thought . . . I mean, I hoped after I told her that Peter was still waiting for her . . . Wait, then how did you know she was dead?"

"Because you're right. She came to see Peter, and then . . ." She looked up at the dark, starry sky. "She saw the light, but she didn't want to leave without him. She took his hand, and the next moment, they were both gone."

"And you didn't go with them? Why?"

She looked at me with a bitter smile. "To walk into the light you have to see it. And I didn't. Because that light wasn't for me. You of all people should know that."

"As you already know, I'm pretty new to all this. So I'd appreciate it if you helped me understand a few things. You said it wasn't your light. Then if that light was Dolly's, how come Peter could cross over with her?"

"If Peter was able to leave with her, it means he saw the light too. And I'm not surprised. The only thing keeping him here was Dolly. "

I bit my lip and nodded. "I'm glad they could do it together. I just wish I could tell her how sorry I am that I couldn't protect her."

"She knows. She left a message for you. She said to tell you it wasn't your fault. That you had no idea what you were up against or how to fight it. She said she's sure that eventually, you'll find a way to destroy them."

With a deep sigh, I turned my eyes up. Looking into the depths of the sky, I murmured, "I will. I promise."

I ARRIVED BACK AT LILY HOUSE, AND AS I STOPPED THE CAR, THE headlights caught a man sitting on the porch steps. Riven.

"Hey. Where have you been? I thought we were searching the woods tonight."

My stomach twisted in knots, I walked to the porch and sat next to him. "Dolly is dead."

"What?" Disbelief colored his voice. "Keira, what happened?"

"She was possessed by that thing. She was possessed and I didn't even notice." I clenched my teeth in frustration.

"Then how you can be sure?"

"I figured it out a few hours ago. I remembered the strange, overwhelming feeling I had in her house the day she invited me for dinner." I heaved a deep breath. "By the time I arrived, it was too late."

"Keira, I'm so sorry. But there was nothing you could've done, even if you'd figured it out earlier. If you tried, you would've only killed Dolly faster."

"I know." I nodded, looking into nowhere. "I saw the spirit leave her body, and I used magic to stop it. But even with all the powerful currents I used on it, it still managed to get away."

"You knew it wouldn't be easy to deal with that thing. It will take time—"

"I told her I would take care of it," I said quietly. "When she realized who I was, she asked if I was here because the scary things from the past were happening again, and I told her I was here to make sure they wouldn't. I let her down."

"No, you can't do this to yourself," Riven said firmly. "You can't blame yourself for her death. Esther knew what those spirits were, where they came from, and how to kill them, but she still had no idea how to destroy them after they possessed someone. For you, who a couple of weeks ago didn't even know the spirits existed, it will take time to figure things out."

"That's the thing. I shouldn't be starting from the beginning. She should've left some records, a grimoire, or a journal. Something," I squeezed the last word out angrily through my teeth.

"I'm sure she did. You just haven't found it yet. Listen, how about we go to my pub? You could use a drink and some distraction."

"No, thanks. I want to see the sheriff in the morning, and I don't want to look hungover."

"What do you need to see the sheriff for?"

"I locked up Dolly's house after the ambulance left. I want to hand over the keys and then stop by the hospital and see if they've reached her son Tony. Maybe I could help him with the funeral arrangements."

"Right. Well." He got up. "I hope you get some sleep, and if you need me, don't hesitate to call."

The moment Riven walked away, I heard Penny's voice behind me. "Dolly is dead?"

"Yes." I pulled myself up, turned around, and met her wide eyes staring back at me. "What are you doing here? I thought you were reading." I went inside.

"I couldn't." She followed me. "I saw you run to the car, and I knew something was wrong. So I waited for you to come back to see if you were okay. Keira," she lowered her voice to nearly a whisper, "are you okay?"

"No. And I'm sure you heard everything, so please, no more questions." I headed straight to my bedroom.

"Okay." With her hands clenched together over her stomach, she remained in the hallway, watching me climb up the stairs.

Without taking off my clothes, I dropped onto the bed, and as my head hit the pillow, the scent of the fresh bedsheets reached my nose. Out of respect for Penny's efforts to keep this place clean, I got up again, took off my boots, then my pants, and slid under the covers.

Every time I closed my eyes, the image of the body covered with a white sheet from my dream last night flickered in front of me. Did this mean that my dream came true? No. At least, not yet. In my dream, I was in Atlanta, and the hospital looked familiar, and there was also this feeling in my gut telling me that the body on the gurney wasn't Dolly's.

So if Dolly wasn't the one from my dream, did it mean someone else was about to die?

I thought of the banshee and her warning. What if she showed up again tomorrow, and the next day, and the day after that? I had no desire for her wail to become my lullaby.

Then I remembered how she acted tonight, the way she bowed her head and vanished after I shouted at her. As if she obeyed my order. She couldn't have. I'd never seen banshees in my life and was probably misreading the whole thing.

My agonizing thoughts kept me awake until dawn. I had to get some sleep, and I grabbed onto the one image that could give my mind peace: the image of Dolly and Peter, hand in hand, walking toward the bright light.

CHAPTER 17

The sheriff's office was located on the first floor of a two-story building in the center of town. I glanced at the small parking lot with a couple of patrol cars and a van on the side of the building, then drove closer to the main entrance and parked next to the dark gray SUV with the words "Whispering Pines SHERIFF" across its doors.

I approached the glass doors under a stone archway and walked inside. There was no one at the front desk. But in the room behind it, I saw a young deputy sitting in front of a computer and showing something to an older man in uniform.

"Hello," I said.

The older man turned around, and I saw the sheriff's badge on his chest.

The deputy was about to get up, but the sheriff put his hand on his shoulder, said, "I got this, you keep looking," and headed toward me. "Hi. What can I help you with?"

"I am—"

"Let me guess," the sheriff interrupted me, and his kind, round eyes smiled. "You must be the young lady staying in Lily House. Keira Hale."

Why bother to try to introduce myself?

"Yep." I pursed my lips, nodding. "That's me."

"Sorry," he said, reading my annoyed reaction. "It's my job, you know." He rounded the front desk and held out his hand. "Sheriff Monroe. I'm glad to finally meet you, Miss Hale."

As we shook hands, he pointed toward the open door of his office. "Please, let's sit down."

The office wasn't big, but it had enough space for a desk, a couple of chairs, a few file cabinets, and a small sofa under the wall. The sheriff took his place behind the desk, and I sank onto the chair across from him.

"So, how do you like Whispering Pines, Miss Hale? I hope you've settled down all right."

Right. Small talk first. "Yes, thank you."

"Good to know. So you're not in any trouble, I hope?"

"No, Sheriff. Everything is fine."

"Then what brings you here, Miss Hale?"

"It's about Dolly Benson. You must've heard that . . . that she died yesterday."

"Yes." The sheriff sighed. "Poor Dolly. She seemed so healthy. If I'm not mistaken, you were the one who found her."

"Yes. I went to visit and found her on the floor. I called the ambulance, and after they took away the body, I locked the door. So I just wanted to hand over the keys." I pulled the keys out of my purse and put them on the desk.

"Thank you, that was very thoughtful of you."

"Sheriff, do you know if the hospital contacted her son?"

"No, not the hospital. We did." He sighed again, rested his hands on the table, and interlocked his fingers. "Tony was a troubled kid. Nothing like his parents. And after he left. . . . Let's say we haven't seen much of him. I'm afraid he won't be able to attend his mother's funeral. You see, he's in jail. For robbery."

My heart sank from the thought of how lonely Dolly must've felt. I never asked her about her son, and now I was glad I didn't.

"I would like to help with the funeral. Financially. And with the arrangements."

"You would?" The sheriff's eyes narrowed. "You were that close to her?"

"I visited her a few times, and she was very friendly and . . ." My guilty conscious was showing, and I had to say something, to give him a better reason for my wish to contribute. "She was a friend of my mom."

"Your mom?" The sheriff frowned slightly, and his eyes fixed at the desk for a moment like he was trying to remember something, and then this knowing smile crossed his face. "You're Esther Millweard's daughter, aren't you?"

I nodded again.

"We haven't seen much of her either since she moved. I hope she is doing ok—"

"She died a few years after she left Whispering Pines."

"Oh, I'm so sorry." Genuine compassion crossed his face.

"Well." I got up to avoid more questions. "I better go. There's a lot to do. I think I'll stop by the hospital first."

"Miss Hale," the sheriff got to his feet as well. "Have you ever done this before?"

"Funerals?" *Good question.* My mom died when I was just a kid, and Simon was the one who made all the arrangements for Dad's funeral. "No." *I'll manage. People do it every day. How hard can it be? I'll Google it.*

"As a sheriff, it's my duty to help in cases like this. We'll provide you with the necessary information. And I'll assign one of my deputies to assist you."

"Thanks. That would be great." I started toward the door but then stopped again. "Sheriff, I would like to keep my financial support anonymous."

He nodded. "If you wish so."

The deputy put together a to-do list for me, and it didn't take long to check off the assignments.

I didn't need to buy a burial plot for Dolly. Her grave place was already reserved next to Peter's. I accepted the deputy's assistance in contacting the church, and we went to make a deal with the minister together.

Then I bought the casket and ordered the flowers to be delivered at the right time. When the funeral date was set, the deputy took care of the announcement in the local newspaper. I ordered a gravestone similar to Peter's, and it was promised to be ready in a month.

Riven showed up a couple of times during those days, offering his help. I appreciated the gesture, but I didn't want him to be seen in town. I assured him I had everything under control and promised to meet him when this was all over.

Three days later, Dolly was properly buried.

About fifteen people came to say goodbye to her. I didn't want much attention, so I stood several graves away with Kate hovering next to me.

"I wonder if they realize she's not there anymore?" said Kate.

"Sure they do. But it doesn't matter. It's still her body and the same face that smiled at them. I'm sure she's looking down at them right now and appreciates their being here, coming to show their respect to the Dolly they knew."

When people started leaving, I headed to my car too.

"It was a nice thing you did for Dolly," said a familiar voice behind me.

I glanced back. "Hey, Martha. What makes you think it was me?"

"Who else would it be? Loved the flowers." She gave me a smile. "You did good, Keira. Your mom would've been proud of you," she said and walked away.

I stood looking after her. Dolly had said once that Martha was one of those who remembered Mom and knew of her special abilities. But something about the way Martha mentioned her made me think she knew more about Mom than Dolly. What made her pretend all this time that she didn't?

Fifteen minutes later, I was sitting on the bar stool next to Riven in his pub. Jackson poured whiskey into two shot glasses and put them in front of us.

I reached for one and raised it. "To Dolly."

"To Dolly," said Riven, picking up the second glass.

Jackson filled our glasses up again as we drained them.

"How did it go?" asked Riven.

"Well, Martha said I did good." I chuckled. "That's a top mark in my book."

"I bet it is," Riven smirked. "Martha is something. She sees everything, knows everything. You can't hide from that old witch."

"I'm sure every small town has its Martha." I picked up my drink. "To Martha." We chinked our glasses and drained them, and only then did Riven's last words click into place. I stared at him. "Sorry, old what?"

"Did I forget to mention that?" He tilted his head.

"If she was a witch, I would've sensed it."

"I bet she knew you would. She must've shielded herself from you somehow."

"Martha was the first person I met when I arrived at Whispering Pines. To shield herself before she even met me, she had to know I was coming."

"Maybe she did know. Like I said, she's a witch."

That wasn't a good enough reason for me, but I didn't elaborate.

"Why would she hide from me?"

"She probably thought . . ." He paused, then changed his

mind. "You know what? Why guess? You'll only get the right answer if you ask her yourself."

"Would I? I mean, get the right answer. How powerful is she?"

"If you mean . . . Oh, no," Riven shook his index finger. "She isn't that kind of witch. She keeps mostly to potions and tarot cards."

"Martha? Tarot cards?" I aimed my pupils at my nose bridge.

Riven chuckled and went on. "She can set up a ward if needed. But she doesn't like her witch side to be advertised, so there are only a few people who know."

"Let's keep it that way. Let her think I have no clue. I'll play her game and see where it takes us."

"We should drink to that. Jackson!"

We both laughed.

Jackson filled our glasses and left the bottle on the counter for us. "You don't need me for this." He grinned. "Not while you can still hit it yourself."

"I don't think Martha being a witch is the only thing you forgot to tell me," I said after another shot. "I heard a rumor that Peter was killed by a werefox." I raised a brow. "If that's true, then you would've known it, wouldn't you?"

"Excuse me?" Riven frowned at me. "A werefox? Being a hunter and all, shouldn't you know that wolves and foxes don't get along?"

"I do. But I don't know any other portal to another realm in this town, and if I remember it right, you told me this is a safe place and you've got everything under control. So how on earth did she manage to come out this door without you being aware of it?"

"I can assure you, we don't have any werefoxes in our realm, so I'm pretty sure it was just that—a rumor." He gave me a leery look. "And who the heck did you hear it from?"

"No one you know." I held up my empty glass for him to fill up.

"I know everyone around here." He grabbed the bottle.

"Okay. Then it's no one you can talk to."

"Oh, God." He chortled. "Don't tell me you heard it from your ghost."

"No. That ghost wasn't mine. And it's long gone now." I raised my glass. "To the departed souls."

By the time I headed home, I was pretty tipsy, but I still managed to walk straight until the moment I shut the pub's door behind me.

The last time I got drunk was after that woman in Atlanta got hit by my magic and ended up in a coma. But I should've known that alcohol wouldn't make the feeling of guilt from Dolly's death disappear.

"I see the funeral went well," Penny muttered, supporting me as I stumbled on the stairs.

"I'm not that drunk, you know. I can get to my bedroom all by myself."

"That's what drunk people usually say. How did you even drive in this state?"

"Magic." I waved my hand triumphantly and dropped on the bed.

"Shoes off! Shoes off!" She grabbed my boot and pulled.

"Penny, did you know that Martha is a witch?"

"Martha is a witch?" She kept losing her grip on the boot. It took her five attempts to get it off my foot. "That sly nag."

I was sure she would've taken off my clothes as well if she could manage.

I reached for the second boot and took it off to save Penny from all the *hard work*.

She tucked me in, turned off the light, and muttered under her breath, "She'll be fine. I'll check on her every five minutes," as she drifted away.

A moment later, through my half-open eyes, I saw her

turn on the lamp next to the armchair and land on its seat with an open book in her hands.

I'm too tired to speak right now. I'll do it tomorrow. Tomorrow I'll tell her off and put her in detention for breaking the rule again.

I watched her turn the page with her cute, transparent fingers, and, smiling, I closed my eyes.

CHAPTER 18

The room was drenched in sunlight, which meant it was almost noon. It was hot, and like it wasn't bad enough I slept in my clothes, last night Penny covered me with a blanket, which was on the floor now, no surprise.

I took off my pants and my sweaty T-shirt and headed to the bathroom to take a shower.

"How are you feeling?" Penny's voice called from the bedroom down the hall.

How did she hear me? I'm not even wearing shoes.

"I'm fine. Keep reading."

I was angry. With myself.

I couldn't save Dolly, or kill the spirit, and it was now out there probably possessing someone else.

I never had a problem catching supernaturals. It might take a day, max three, for me to find a portal in Atlanta, or anywhere else I worked before.

And now . . . I'd never felt so helpless.

Nothing I'd learned so far brought me any closer to finding the answer to the two most important questions: where was the portal the spirits were using and how could I destroy them? Instead, I got another one: why were they so interested in some bloody gate? Unless . . . *Wait a minute. Maybe the gate* is *their portal?* I sneered at the thought. *And they what, forgot where it is and want me to find it for them?*

I stood under the water with my eyes closed and once again went through my conversation with Dolly, or with who I thought was Dolly, at the dinner. The spirit wanted to know if I got any new information from Laura. Then it asked me about the gate, and when I said I didn't know anything about it yet, the spirit seemed surprised. It thought that Mom must've left clues for me.

Oh, God. I was right. The gate is *their portal.*

What confused me was thinking the spirits were trying to find that damn gate, or I would've realized sooner it was the other way around.

The gate must be their portal, and they're trying to find out if Mom left me information on its location. They're afraid I'll find it and send them back.

Was that why they killed Mom? Because she was going to send them back? If so, why was I still alive?

After I dried my hair, I put on a fresh tank top, and since there was not a single cloud in the sky, I ditched the pants, put on my jeans shorts, and went to the kitchen. I was hungry. The last thing I ate was a protein bar yesterday at three p.m.

I made myself a fat sandwich. Just as I took the first bite, Penny flew in and opened the cupboard. She pulled out a mug, filled it with coffee, and put it in front of me.

"Thanks." I looked with suspicion at her as she landed on the chair across from me, beaming. "What's up?"

"Nothing." She shrugged.

"Really?" I raised a brow. "Then what are you so happy about?"

"Ooooh, okay." Looking excited, she leaned forward. "It's Rosalee. You see, Jerald was dating her sister, but he fell in love with Rosalee the moment he met her. But he was still going to marry her sister because she said she was pregnant. Now Rosalee found out that her sister faked her pregnancy and she only wanted to marry Jerald because he's a billionaire. Can you imagine if Jerald finds out?"

I almost choked on my sandwich. "Are you talking about your book?"

"Yeah." Penny's smile froze.

Well, at least one of us is having fun.

"So you like the story, I take it?" I smiled to bring her cheer back.

"Yes. This book," she beamed again, "it's such a page-turner. Thank you for getting it for me, Keira."

"Hey, you happy makes me happy."

"Aww." She flew around me, hovered behind my chair and gave me a hug.

Oh, God. Kill me now.

Her grip wasn't as tight as she intended it to be, but I could still feel her cold but soft touch.

"Penny, I'm eating." I clapped her arm wrapped around my neck so she would let go. But it didn't seem to have any effect on her. The fact she could grab things didn't make her corporeal. As a result, my hand went through her arm and I ended up clapping my own shoulder.

"I wish I had a big library," she sighed.

"And I wish I had a flying carpet."

She chuckled next to my ear and finally let go of me.

"Do you have plans for today?" she asked as I swallowed the last piece of my sandwich and washed it down with a few gulps of coffee.

"Yep. The water in the pond is evaporating much faster than I hoped it would."

"Yeah." Penny sighed again.

"I want to find out if someone else has a pond in this

town and see if they're having the same problem. Then I might visit Laura."

"Visit Laura? Again?" she asked, looking puzzled. "Why?"

I jerked my shoulder. "Just to check on her."

After what happened to Dolly, I started to fear for Laura's safety even though her case was completely different. I didn't want anyone else to die on my watch, if I could help it. I also wondered if she had heard anything about the gate.

MARTHA WAS TALKING TO A YOUNG WOMAN WITH A TODDLER IN her arms next to the baby food aisle. The two of them didn't notice me come in, so I walked down the aisle on the other side of the store to give them some time to finish their conversation and ended up staring at the different kinds of toilet paper and paper towel rolls. I reached the end of the aisle, turned to the right, and almost collided with an elderly man staring at the fridge with drinks.

I rounded the man, and as I walked down the next aisle, I heard the young woman's voice.

"I met Sheriff Monroe at the clinic the other day and I asked him about Tony. If he'd get permission to plan his mother's funeral," the woman said. "But the sheriff said Tony wouldn't be able to make it. So who planned it? Who buried poor Dolly?"

I pricked up my ears. Dolly had said once that even though Martha was pretty chatty, she wouldn't tell people more than she should.

"The important thing is that it's done. And done nicely," Martha replied. "I'm sure Dolly would've loved it."

I heard them move toward the cash register and I too headed back toward the entrance.

"Yeah, you're right," the woman said. "I was just curious—"

"Hey, there." I showed myself to put an end to her curiosity.

Martha turned around. "Keira, hi."

The woman looked out from behind Martha. "Hi." She smiled.

Martha stepped behind the counter. She loaded the woman's groceries into the paper bag, and as the woman paid and headed to the door, Martha waved to the toddler looking back at her over his mother's shoulder. "Bye, Kevin."

"I'm not here for shopping," I said as she raised her eyebrows at my empty hands.

"I see. Then what can I help you with?" Martha tilted her head, looking intrigued.

"I have a quick question."

"Shoot." She folded her arms over her chest.

"Do you know if anyone in town has a pond?"

"A pond?" She stared at me.

"Yes. There's something wrong with the Lily House pond, and I thought—"

"What's wrong with it?" Martha interrupted me, her expression growing serious.

"It's drying out."

Her hands fell to her sides. "What?"

"Is it bad? I mean, I know it's bad, but—"

"Oh, believe me, it's bad." Frowning, she pierced me with a gaze. "Don't bother to ask around. No one can help you."

Her reaction confused me. I gazed back at her. "What do you mean?"

"I mean," she said, sounding even more cryptic, "if it's already happening, you can't stop it."

"No, I realize there isn't much I can do if it's drying. I was just wondering if the same thing is happening to the other ponds. The owners would know what's causing it if this has happened before, wouldn't they?"

"You're wondering what's causing it," Martha scoffed, shaking her head.

This reaction puzzled me even more. "Yeah. Why's that funny?"

"Trust me, it's not. But like I said, you'll be wasting your time. They can't help you."

I had the feeling this was Martha the witch talking to me right now. "Are we still talking about the pond?" I narrowed my eyes.

She looked away. "Yes. Isn't it what you were asking about?" She absentmindedly pushed back the paper bags sticking out of the pile.

Something wasn't right here, and I wasn't going to leave until I got some answers.

"Martha, what's going on? If you know something, you need to tell me."

Looking anywhere but at me, she shrugged. "There's nothing to tell."

I rounded the counter, clenched my hand around her wrist, and muttered, "*Confractus*."

The blast of energy shot through the store, shaking the shelves. Martha's magic blocking shield was broken.

I tilted my head. "How about now?"

"Who told you?" She glared at me. "Was it Riven?"

"That was one powerful shield, Martha."

"This doesn't change anything."

"No? Then why put it up at all? Why were you hiding from me?"

She jerked her hand out of my grip. "Because I knew you'd come asking questions I couldn't give answers to. Not because I don't want to, but because I'm not the right person to do so."

"Do you know who the right person is?"

"I might . . . but . . ." She bit her lip.

"Martha." I scowled at her. "I need help to understand what's happening here."

"Okay, okay," she barked, letting out her frustration. "Give me until tomorrow. I'll see what I can do." She glanced toward the shelving at the back of the store. "Charles," she called, "are you alive there?"

The elderly man I'd completely forgotten about shuffled out from between the aisles. "What the hell was that?" he grumbled.

"Just a little quake. But you're okay, aren't you?" she asked, her tone returning to normal.

"I'm fine." He put two bottles of beer and a can of beans he was holding in his hands down on the counter.

Without another glance at Martha, I said, "See you tomorrow," and strode to the door.

What the bloody hell was that all about?

My head still processing the conversation, I got in the car and started the engine. What was it that Martha knew but couldn't tell me? And what did it have to do with the pond?

CHAPTER 19

The mental health center lobby was just as quiet as the previous time. After I signed my name in the journal, I was approached by the same nurse.

"Miss Hale, it's so nice of you to visit Laura again," she said as we walked down the hallway.

"Wasn't Laura's room that way?" I pointed at the turn we took the last time.

"Oh, she's not in her room. This way, please."

She led me into a room full of patients.

"I've been working here for six years, and I don't remember her ever leaving her room. But a couple of days after your visit, she asked me to take her here." The nurse nodded toward the left corner, where Laura sat at a small table.

"She did?" After all the bad things that had happened, this little news brightened my mood. "Why is she in a wheelchair? Is there a problem with her legs?"

"No. She does walk around her room. For someone who's been by herself for such a long time, she must feel the need to have something familiar with her. I think her wheelchair makes her feel safe in this new environment. But

I'm sure, given some time," the nurse smiled at me, "and maybe a couple more of your visits, she'll get rid of that too."

"I'll try my best." I nodded.

Laura was playing solitaire. Her eyes were fixed on the cards, and she didn't see me coming. She only looked up when I pulled the vacant chair from under the wall and sat across from her.

"Keira?" A smile spread across her face. "I hoped you'd come."

"Hi, Laura." I smiled back. "How're you doing?"

"As you can see, I took your advice and got out of my room."

"How does it feel? Did it make any difference?"

"Oh, yes. I try to keep busy, like you advised." Her gaze slid down to the cards in her hand. "I did a puzzle. They've got a few here, but the pieces were big and it was too easy even for someone old like me. The cards are better. The layout is always different, so it keeps my interest, and I can play this game as many times as I want. And you were right. This thing . . ." She glanced around and lowered her voice. "It can't get into my head as easily when I'm here."

"But it still does?"

"Yeah, mostly when I'm back in my room. But thanks to you, I feel so much better." Her lips curved upward, deepening the lines around her eyes.

"I'm glad I could help."

There was a nurse, a tall, strong man, sitting at a small table next to the door. He was watching the patients and me. I was the only visitor in the room, and I supposed it was his job to make sure I was safe.

"How are you, Keira? Did you get any closer to finding a way to get rid of this thing?"

"Not yet. It'll take some time. Sorry. I wish I had better news for you, but unfortunately, there's another one out there, and I need to deal with him before he possesses someone else."

"In Whispering Pines?"

"Yes."

"When you say *possesses someone else,* does that mean it has possessed someone recently?"

"Yes. Dolly."

"Dolly Benson?" Laura gasped. "What happened? Is it still inside her?"

"No." I shook my head. "She died a few days after it happened. We buried her yesterday."

"Oh, God, poor Dolly. I can't believe those things are still out there."

"To fight them, I need to learn as much about them as I can, so I need to ask you something. Has the spirit ever mentioned anything about a gate?"

Laura pondered for a moment.

"No," she said. "Nothing about a gate that I can remember. Is it important?"

"It has to be, because they seem pretty interested in it. I think this gate . . ." I glanced around to make sure no one was listening to our conversation. "I think it's how they get here. Through some gate. Maybe if I find it—"

Laura let out a rasping laugh, and her green eyes turned pitch black. "So you don't know where it is? That's a relief."

A couple of patients looked around for the source of the rough voice.

The anger boiled my blood. "What are you so happy about?" I sneered.

"We killed Esther because we thought it would help. It didn't. But you did. You've already pulled the trigger. We can feel it. And because you've no idea what you're dealing with, you won't be able to stop what's coming. Even if you knew, it's too late now."

"Too late for what? What are you talking about?"

The spirit didn't answer but laughed again. This time, a couple of patients turned their heads, throwing suspicious looks our direction. Luckily, Laura was sitting with her back to the rest of the room. No one saw her face, and as the man at the door got to his feet, I pretended to laugh too, like we were making fun of something.

Still watching us, the man sank back into his chair.

Keeping my voice down, I said, "Trust me, I'll figure this out, and we'll see who's laughing in the end. Maybe I can't kill you right now, but you're still imprisoned, and you'll stay imprisoned much longer—"

"Longer—yes. Much . . ." Laura, who wasn't Laura right now, shook her head. "Let me rephrase your words. *Not* much longer. This body is old. She isn't going to live forever. And mark or no mark—the moment she dies, I'll be free."

Laura's body jerked slightly a few times, like she was trying to shake something off.

"Oh, God," she said in her real voice. "Did it just. . . ?"

"Yes," I whispered. "But don't worry, no one saw anything. Laura, I'm sure it happened because of me. My question provoked him, so I better go before it happens again. I'm sorry."

"Don't be. Didn't you say the other day that this was a fight? You said you need to learn how to deal with them. If this is the way, then so be it."

There were two things that I learned from this short visit. The first was that the spirits were indeed afraid of me finding the gate. And the second—the spirit that was trapped inside Laura would get its freedom back the moment she died, which had not occurred to me before.

The portal to Riven's realm was just like any other portal, and finding it was easy. All I needed was my magic. But it was different with the gate. I was sure that damn gate the spirits came through was somewhere here in Whispering Pines, and the fact that I still had no clue where to look for it meant it wasn't an ordinary portal. I had a suspicion that finding it would require not only the exact knowledge of its location but also a different kind of magic.

When I returned to Lily House, I went to my room, picked up Mom's picture from the dresser, and sat on the bed.

Laura's spirit said they killed Mom hoping it would help. Help with what? And that I pulled the trigger? What trigger? And how did I do that?

The scariest part was that it said it was too late to undo what I did. And how could I undo something if I didn't know what it was I did in the first place?

"There's so much I don't understand," I murmured under my breath, running my thumb over Mom's image. "You knew that my life would depend on this knowledge, and I'm sure you left it for me in one form or another in case something happened to you. I promise I'll find it. I'll figure this out."

My phone buzzed in my pocket. I pulled it out and saw Simon's name on the screen.

"Hey, little brother."

"Hi, Keira. How are you?"

"I'm fine. And you?" I asked. "Simon, did something happen?" I held my breath.

"No. At least nothing bad. There's news, though. The lawyer came by to read Dad's will to the family. Which meant me, and I wished you were here so we could do this together."

"Simon." I heaved a breath. "I'm sorry."

He sighed too. "Don't worry. Luckily, it wasn't that long. Dad left everything fifty-fifty for the two of us. So you're rich now. Do you want the details?" I could tell he was grinning.

"Oh, God, no." I chuckled. "You know them, and that's

enough for me. Simon, thank you for taking care of things." I added quietly, "I miss you, and I would be there if I could. But I need to get this done. I need to finish what Dad started."

"I know, sis. I just needed to hear your voice. To make sure you're okay."

I heard a car outside. I turned and looked toward the window. From where I sat, all I saw was the top of the gate and a taxi pulling away.

"Keira," Penny called from behind the door, excitement in her voice.

"What is it, Penny?"

"He's here."

"Who?" I got up from the bed and stepped to the window. As I looked down at the yard, I caught a glimpse of a tall, well-built man before he disappeared under the porch's roof. "Sorry, Simon, I gotta go."

"Keira, promise you'll call if you need help."

"I promise, little brother." But of course, that was a lie. After I'd learned the truth about what happened to his parents, I would never involve him in this case.

The next moment, I heard the front door open with a bang.

Did that son of a bitch just kick my door? I dropped my phone on the bed, grabbed my gun from the dresser, and hurried to the foyer.

"There she is." The man scowled at me when he saw me coming down the stairs.

Tall and handsome with short black hair, dressed in a black shirt and gray slacks, he looked like he'd just walked off a photoshoot for a whiskey commercial.

"Polite people knock." I pierced his coal-black eye sockets with my glare. "But you're not human, are you?" I reached the bottom of the stairs. Keeping my distance, I pointed at him my gun. "You're a demon."

"And you're what? A unicorn?" He scoffed.

"No. I'm a hunter, and I'm about to make a hole in your head."

Penny darted forward and hung in mid-air between us. Covering him protectively with her transparent body, she stared at me with wide eyes.

"No. No, Keira, you don't understand," she sputtered, waving her hands. "That's *him.*"

"You mean *him* him?"

"Yeah." She nodded frantically.

"Penny," the demon growled. "Get your butt off my face."

"Oh, sorry." Penny dashed to the side.

"Don't talk to her like that," I barked, still aiming my gun at him. Touched by my protective reaction, Penny released a little squeak. "So what?" I looked at them, from the demon to Penny and back. "You're saying you can see and hear her?"

"Of course I can see and hear her." He rolled his eyes.

Of course, he can. If that's *him,* then he's the one who put her here to look after the house.

So it wasn't Dad she was talking about.

"You know that thing isn't going to kill me." The demon marched toward me, jerked the gun out of my hand, and tossed it aside. "Do you have any idea what you've done?" He glared at me with fury, and his black, bottomless eye sockets turned into sparkling embers.

"I don't know what you mean," I hissed, returning the glare. "But I have the feeling you're about to tell me.

ALSO BY LANA MELYAN

QUEEN OF GATES

Magic In Me (Book 2)

Demon In Me (Book3)

FORGED BY FATE

Wolf Cursed (Book 1)

Hybrid Born (Book 2)

Heir Chosen (Book 3)

THE WEIGHT OF MAGIC

1.The First Wave

2.The Legacy

3.The First Spell

4.The Family Tree

5.The First Fight

6.The Last Bell

7.The Sacrifice

8.The Last Secret

9.The Call of Blood

THE ETERNITY ROAD

Trilogy

The First Hunter (Book 1)

The Return (Book 2)

The Keeper of the Book (Book 3)

BELLSANDSPELLS

Romantic Christmas Novella

Visit Lana Melyan's website lanamelyan.com to subscribe to the mailing list and to be the first to learn about new releases and discounts.